# HUNTED BY FIRE

STEPHANIE E. DONOHUE

Published by Never and Ever Publishing https://neverandeverbooks.com/

Edited by Meg Dailey https://thedaileyeditor.wordpress.com/

Map created by Hannah at Centaur Maps https://linktr.ee/centaurmaps

Cover by S.E.D Creations

https://sedcreation.com/

UCHEN
SAKAR
IDRIL
DUNBAR
ASHBORNE
FURNESS
NORHALL
THORNE
LENWICK
ONRYX
LUNDY
DETHA
AECKLAND
EXETER
DAIGH
SOLARIS
OAKWELL
KELD
NASCOMBE
NERDANEL
KALD
APRA
MORTHAM
SALKIRE
ECHA
MULNIGAN SEA
VATRA
MUIRIN
LAEWAES
DARFIELD
KILERTH
ILRAGORN
HARTHWAITE
VAPORIA
SWINDON
VICTARION
PANTMAWE
NIALL
HADLEIGH
NETHERIDGE
GLENARM
BULLMAR
SANADRIN
MARREN
ECKIN
LAMEX
EMALL
ARAMORE
DALRY
HARAN
CULLFIELD
JABBART
SHARPTON
SANLOW
ALRYNE
MARACH
PELLA
PIRN
BERKTON
BAFRUS
MIRFIELD
LANDOW
MERTON
CYNERIK
FALLHOLT

# Contents

This book contains violence, graphic descriptions of blood/gore, mentions of sexual assault, mentions of abuse/assault to a minor, and general language. Also includes scenes depicting the loss of family members/loved ones and scenes showcasing mental health issues, including (but not limited to) anxiety and depression.

To anyone who's
ever struggled with
loss, depression, anxiety,
or who has felt like they're
forever stuck on the fringes
of society. I see you. I've been there.

Hang in there…it does get better.

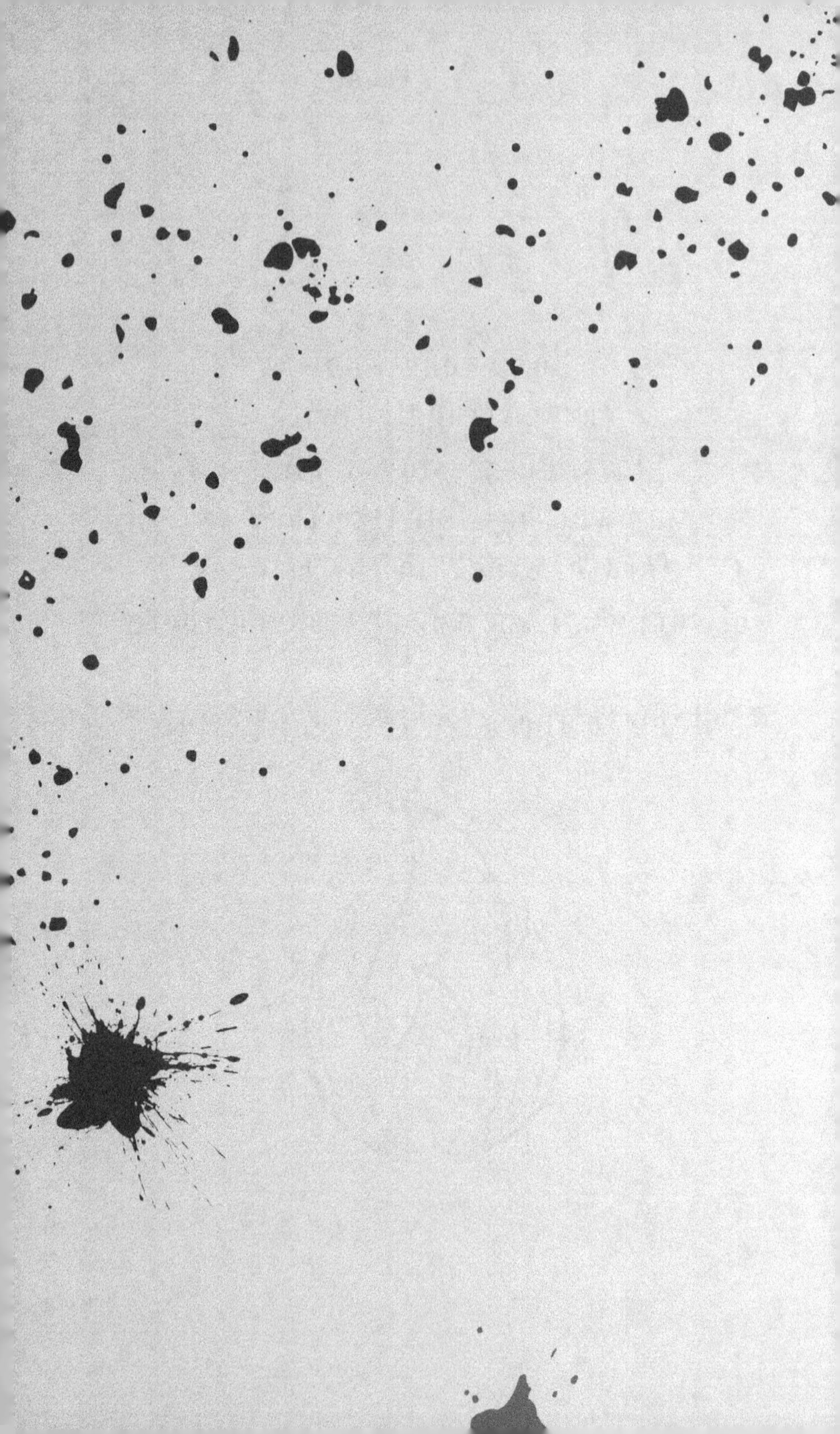

# Beginning

Fire is very humanlike.

It has humble origins—a spark, no bigger than a fingertip. And then it grows. Innocent, at first, but often becoming more ~~malisious~~ malicious as it develops. Anger will cause it to fume and swell. It will consume land greedily but will never be full nor truly satisfied. It is capable of taking life, of causing pain, but also capable of creating.

Very much like humans, yes?

Well, perhaps not *all* humans. But many of them.

I was a babe when I first found myself entranced by a dancing flame. I did not understand what it was, or what it could do. The bitter cold had been rattling my bones all day, and the flame offered warmth.

I stretched my hand out, hoping to bring its heat closer.

Touching it, of course, only led to pain. The fire ~~revenishly~~ —ravenously devoured my skin. I cried, shaking my hand, but the flame refused to give up its meal. Until my mother doused it with water.

The burn on my palm had taken weeks to heal, and I gave fire a wide berth after that.

Until it became a part of me.

I never felt another burn. Instead, I incinerated others. Hundreds—nay, thousands had died by my hands over the years. Some deserved their painful demise. Most were innocent.

Am I remorseful? Of course. But it's a rather pointless emotion; it won't bring them back.

Perhaps you think me a monster. And perhaps I am. I suppose it doesn't matter. I am not ~~righting~~ —*writing* this to receive absolution.

Someone once told me putting my thoughts on paper would—what is the saying? *Uncludder my mind.*

(That doesn't seem right. Uncludder? Or unclutter?)

If anyone is reading this, please bear in mind I only learned how to ~~right~~ —write a few years ago.

And if putting these words to parchment helps to *uncludder* my mind...well, I would like to have a few moments of peace. Especially since I don't know how many moments I have left.

Perhaps I should start at the beginning.

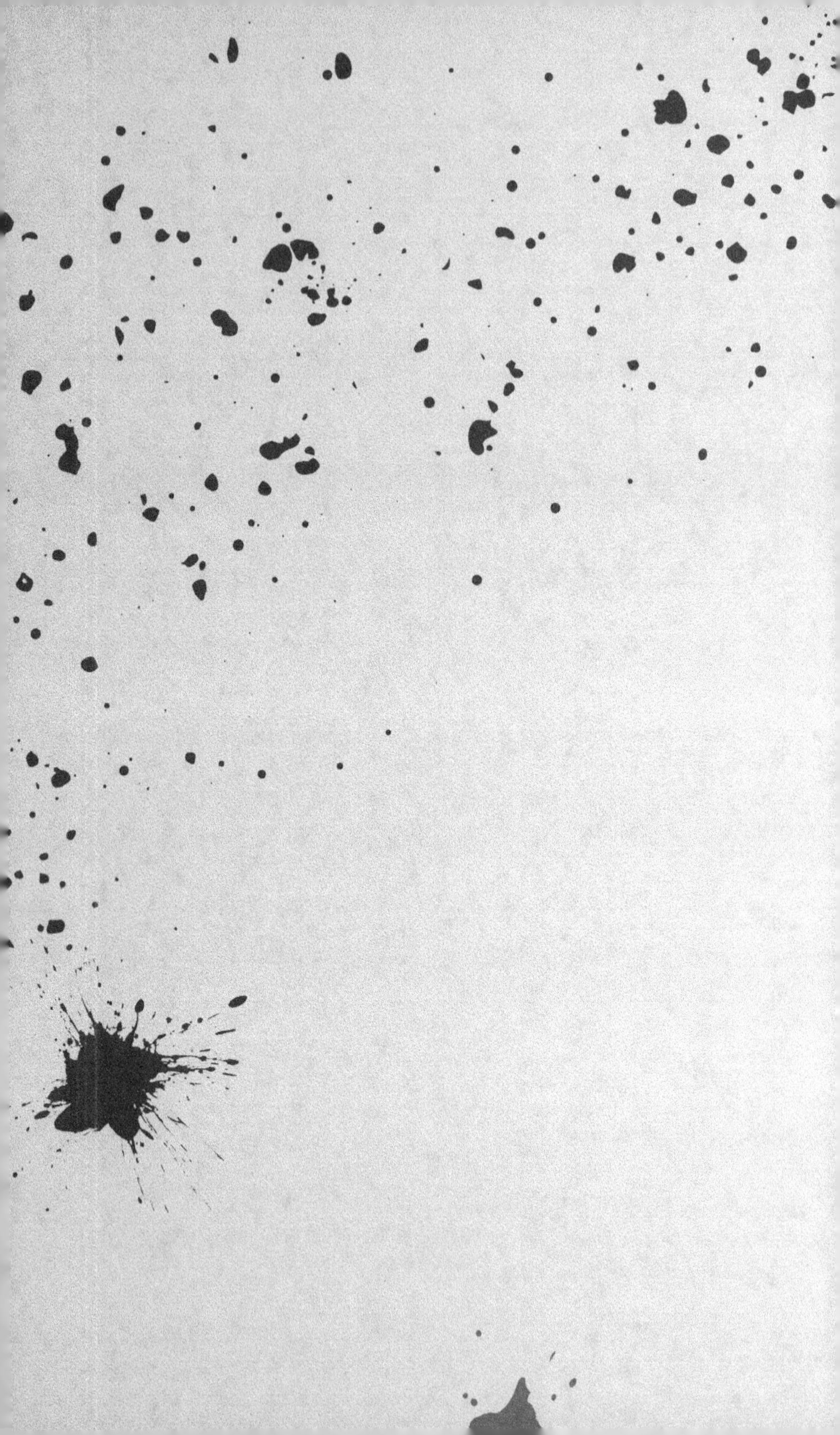

# Varn

Where shall I start?

Scribing the harrowing events of the last few days would likely be enough to fill my bind of parchment. And I don't want to focus on the end of my life; I wish to compile its entirety, as accurately as I can recall it.

I had a name, once. Given to me by my mother when I entered this world. I don't remember it now. And I've been called many things throughout my life, so I doubt I'll ever recall it.

At the time of ~~righting~~ writing this, I am thirty years of age. Or perhaps twenty-nine? I'm uncertain of my age as I don't know when I was born.

It's odd, yes? Most humans know the year, if not the precise day, of their birth. In the olden times, it was customary to view the anniversary of one's birth as a celebration.

But I do not have this knowledge. And thus, I can only guess at my age; I have seen at least three decades on this earth, but I will not live long enough to see my fourth.

I spent the early years of my childhood in a ghastly place

called Detha, one of the many cities in Celestial-ruled Uchen. It is still controlled by Celestials. For all that I have achieved, I could not free my kin, and I never will.

Those fortunate to have never lived in a Celestial-ruled city will not understand the atrocities that occur behind those walls. It's better not to be born at all than to be born in a place such as Detha. Hence why my arrival was not an event to be celebrated.

In Detha, humans were treated as livestock.

No. I apologize, I've made an inaccurate statement.

The livestock were treated *far* better than the humans.

Detha produced food in abundance, but people still starved. The Celestials received our finest crops and cuts of meat, you see. Even though they did not *need* to eat our food, they enjoyed indulging themselves. The Wraiths, enforcers of Celestial law, were offered the second finest crops and meats. Humans were given whatever was left—hardly enough to feed a family, let alone a sprawling city.

The Wraiths of Detha governed with a heavy hand. Punishments were dealt frequently and swiftly for all manner of offenses. For example, sneezing too often could earn a human fifteen whiplashes. Coughing too loudly could result in the removal of a non-important limb—fingers, toes, ears, whatever the Wraith fancied. Failing to make The Offering, the daily basket of food humans prepared for the Celestials, was a death sentence. It didn't matter the reason. Even if a storm ~~desimated~~ decimated a person's crops, or a plague struck their animals, The Offering was still expected. ~~Lein-eeny~~ leniency was only given if the offender had something else to offer.

Another human, perhaps.

Wraiths savored the taste of human. And, although they were not spared the wrath of a Celestial when The Offering was scant, they happily endured the punishment if it allowed them to fill their bellies with human flesh.

I've been told it's our *souls* Wraiths truly crave, as they do not have one of their own. But, as they are incapable of extracting souls, they settle for flesh.

Varn, the odious Wraith who commanded the army, had an ~~instat—insatit~~...(I know how to spell this word, bear with me)...*insatiable*. Varn had an *insatiable* appetite for humans. He even had a favored method of cooking them: crisping their skin, while leaving their innards raw and moist. He also preferred his meals to still be alive when he consumed them. "Death makes the muscles too tough," I'd once heard him say. "But living muscle *melts* on the tongue."

I'm not certain how true that statement is, as I've never had the desire to test it. But I nearly became one of his meals.

I had only walked the earth for six (or five, or seven) years when Mama died. She succumbed to the cough, as did many others that winter. Papa had died of the same affliction two years prior. I don't remember him. Some days I struggle to recall Mama.

During the peak of the winter months, Varn holed himself up inside his house, his gaunt body propped before a roaring fire. He didn't much like the cold, you see. And he did not need to endure it when he had an army to do his bidding.

Varn's duty, his sole purpose for residing in Detha, was to ensure the Celestials were content. And the Celestials were easily contented, as long as they could engorge themselves on our food while simultaneously ignoring our very existence.

So Varn had a simple job: he ordered his soldiers to collect The Offering and keep us *motivated* to continue working.

His soldiers eagerly complied.

On the day Mama died, the Wraiths came to collect The Offering at dusk. They took me instead.

I was amongst five others—two of us were orphaned children, the other three had been Offered—brought to Varn's home that day. The Wraiths herded us into a spacious room where the ceiling seemed high enough to reach the heavens and the floor was made of a reflective material. I received quite a fright when I glanced down and saw my own ~~dishelved~~ disheveled, terror-stricken face staring back at me. I'd never seen my reflection before, and I was rather shocked at how monstrous I looked.

My surprised gasp did not go unnoticed.

"Quiet!" the Wraith beside me shouted. His whip lashed my arm.

I winced as blood pooled from the narrow fissure that formed in my dirt-caked skin and bit my tongue to stifle my cry.

The five of us stood beside a ~~behometh~~ behemoth fireplace while Varn sat at a golden table, his white eyes following our movements.

The first to be roasted was a man named Oisin. I knew him rather well. He and his family tended a herd of cattle near Mama's dwelling. Disease had taken most of his herd. The remaining cows produced little milk and were too thin to slaughter for meat. So he'd Offered himself. His sacrifice gave his family another day to either coax more milk from their cows or find something else to Offer.

I liked Oisin. He used to hum, claiming his cows were soothed by his voice and encouraged to give him more milk.

Now he shook silently, his face pale, eyes shimmering as the Wraiths stripped him of his clothing and strapped him to a spit. His wails reverberated off the high ceiling as his body hovered over the dancing flames. It took only moments for his skin to blister. The rancid odor turned my stomach to rot.

Oisin never ceased screaming. His voice had grown hoarse when the Wraiths pulled his mottled body from the hearth and placed it on Varn's table. Oisin's cries only abated after Varn cut several long strips of meat from his abdomen.

I felt no fear as I watched this unfold. Or, perhaps I did and I don't remember, but I think I had accepted my fate. Death was a familiar friend in Detha.

"Next!" Varn shouted. He heaped several large hunks of skin, muscle, and fat onto a serving platter before passing the remnants of Oisin's body to his soldiers.

A Wraith grasped my shoulder, herding me toward the hearth.

"No, not that one! Too small." Varn spat food as he spoke. "There's no meat on those bones! Throw her on last." Crisped pieces of flesh dangled from his teeth when he smiled.

As it turned out, my slight, underdeveloped body saved my life.

A female Celestial plucked me out of the line as the Wraiths removed a keening woman from the fire; the third human to be placed on Varn's table.

"Don't be afraid." The Celestial's purring voice caused me to shiver. Her breath carried the scent of apples.

The Wraiths shouted in alarm. Varn, blood dribbling down his chin, stood. His golden chair made an awful shriek as it scraped against the floor.

"It's alright," the Celestial said. "Be at ease. There will be no punishment tonight for the meager Offering. But I am taking the girl with me."

It was uncomfortable, the way the Celestial pressed my back against her front and trailed her fingers over my shoulders. For the first time that night, I had an urge to scream.

But we flew away before I could open my mouth.

Of course, Celestials do not fly as birds do. Traveling with her was akin to…well, it's difficult to describe. I suppose it's akin to the hide-and-go-seek games children play. To be more specific: the part of the game where the seeker is blindfolded and spun until they're disoriented.

Once I had returned to solid ground, staring at glistering white walls, and crying because my stomach fluttered, the Celestial grasped my chin in her palms. "Drink," she commanded, pressing a glass vial to my lips. Radiant silver liquid swirled inside the container—her blood.

At the time, I did not know what it was. I merely balked at the scent: like a slab of cheese that had festered in the blistering summer sun.

I dug my teeth into my lips, keeping my mouth closed.

"Drink!" The Celestial pried my jaw open, ignoring my whimper of pain, and tipped the contents of the vial to the back of my throat.

I sputtered, prepared to spit the liquid out, but she clasped a hand over my mouth and pinched my nostrils, suffocating me. Forcing me to swallow.

The pain began immediately.

It felt as though every bone in my body were being broken, reset, and broken again. The sensation lasted for hours, *days*, with me screaming until I had no voice left. I clawed at my skin, digging my nails in so deep, I left welts. I vomited and fouled myself.

The Celestial stayed by my side, but her presence offered no comfort. She never spoke or sang lullabies to ease my torment, nor did she offer me a kind touch. She only shoved bits of food and water into my mouth a few times a day, keeping me alive, even as I pleaded for death.

When a second Celestial arrived, eyes alight with fury, I thought I'd been granted my wish.

Instead, I was taken again, forced to endure the dizzying way Celestials travel for the second time.

Black spots swarmed my vision as we landed. A deep, piercing sound filled my ears, making it impossible to hear anything else. The Celestial, a male this time, gently deposited me in a meadow. He said something, although I couldn't hear anything beyond the shrill noise in my ears. And then he left.

I finished the last dregs of my transformation alone.

Hours later, as the pain ebbed from my bones, I stared at a blue sky. It was still winter, and cold, and the grass had long since turned brown. But a promise of spring teased the air. The sun cast its warmth upon the earth. The breeze smelled of flowers—those that had bloomed early, perhaps hoping the warm days would stay.

I was all alone. Abandoned. And, as I would soon discover, I was no longer human.

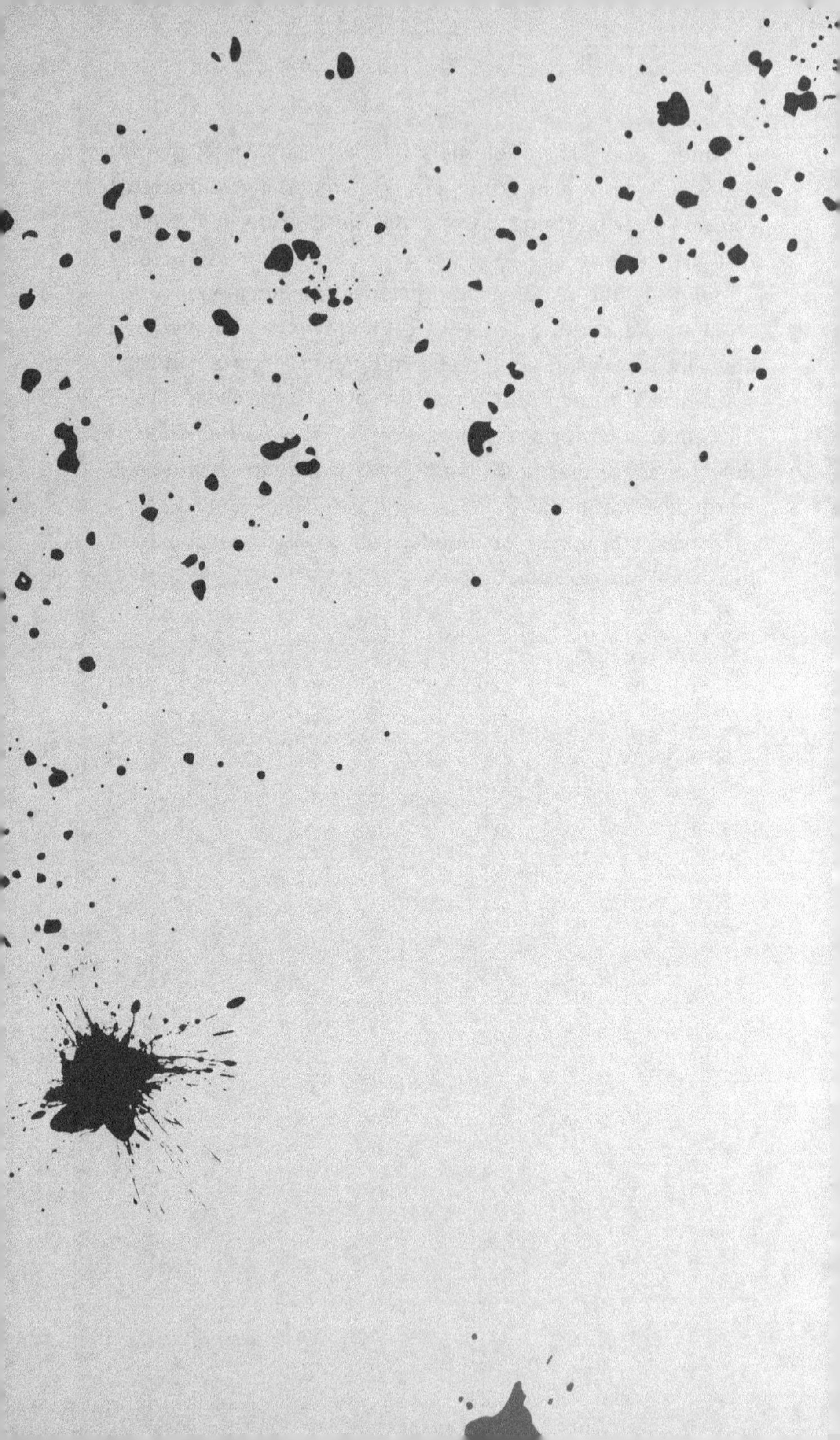

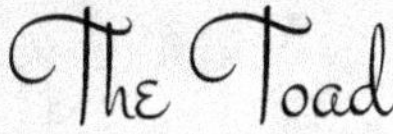

# The Toad

I reached the forest as the sun dipped below the horizon and all traces of spring warmth vanished. The air turned bitterly cold. My clothes were still damp. Whether from the remnants of sweat, bile, or urine, I didn't know.

Above me, branches groaned and whined as the trees swayed in the wind. Animals yowled and slithered through the undergrowth.

My skin prickled as I wandered through the dense wood. A cold, heavy sensation settled into my gut, as though my bowels were cramping. Sweat dripped in a steady rhythm down my back, even as the frigid air cut through my tunic.

I'd never been outside in the dark before. Most humans in Detha weren't permitted to wander outside after sunset. As the Wraiths preferred to spend their evenings indoors (usually feasting on human flesh), only a scant number of guards patrolled our streets in the evenings. And they were less merciful than their daytime counterparts. 'Twas a death sentence for a human to be found outside their dwelling at night without just cause. And few causes were considered *"just"* in the eyes of the Wraiths.

So it was a peculiar thing, being outside at night. In the woods. Alone.

And, when secured in fear's iron grasp, the mind tends to ~~eaggerate~~ exaggerate. The hoot of an owl morphed into the braying shouts of a Wraith. The creaking of bushes became ~~ominious~~ ominous whispering.

I quickened my pace, desperate to find…something. A safe place to hide. A path out of the wretched wood. *Anything.*

The trees swayed again. Flutters of moonlight pierced the deep pools of blackness that had gathered beneath the trunks.

*Rustle, rustle,* went the branches.

I stopped, my belly suddenly feeling as though it were struggling to digest a rather large rock.

*Rustle, rustle.*

The noise seemed eerily similar to the flapping of wings.

Dim gleams of silver flitted across the dark ground before me. A scream rose in my throat, but I clasped a hand over my mouth before I vocalized it.

The pattern of moonlight was fractured. Feathered. As though filtering through a Celestial's wing.

I urged my weary legs into a run. I had no destination in mind, only the desire to put as much distance between myself and the Celestial as possible.

The vegetation thickened as I hurtled deeper into the wood. Thorns and twigs reached for me, their sharp edges digging into my skin, making me gasp. All the while, the branches above me continued to undulate and make that wretched *rustle, rustle* sound.

I only stopped when I emerged in a small clearing. The shadows were not so dark here. The moon provided more illumination. As I braced my hands on my knees and inhaled, my terror ebbed. The rational side of my brain emerged again.

Until the frog croaked.

A rather harmless noise. One that shouldn't have induced such heart-stopping terror in me. But it did. Why? Well, a person dying of the cough will develop a similar rasping sound.

*Raaaph. Raaaphuh.*

"Mama?" I bleated.

*Raaaaphuh,* croaked the frog.

"Mama!"

My feet slid against the grass as I galloped across the clearing. "Mama!"

It was foolish to hope. Mama was dead. I'd watched her demise unfold.

Her illness began gradually.

It started on the day of our first snowfall; always a ~~monumentous~~ momentous occasion. For the children, at least. I'm rather certain the adults felt nothing but fury as they stared at the white flakes. After all, they still had to complete their daily tasks, and the snow hampered their progress.

Mama was no exception.

We lived on a tomato field. The Celestials, of course, manipulated the soil; tricking it into thinking summer never faded—hence why tomatoes still grew, even as ice fell from the sky. The Celestials also gifted us with spools of mesh fabric to protect the plant life from the frigid air.

"'Tis material from the Celestial City, love," Mama had told me that morning as she unfurled the gleaming fabric and draped it over the vines.

I was ~~memorized~~ mesmerized as I ran my fingers over the silken-smooth mesh. But then the snow began swirling with renewed intensity and my focus turned to the layers of fluffy ice coating the ground. Such is the fickle mind of a young child.

Mama began coughing that day.

At first, it was a tickle that struck whenever Mama moved about in the winter air. She would clear her throat, cough a handful of times, and jest that she was developing an aversion to the cold. "Perhaps I'm turning into a Wraith," she said.

The thought was horrifying. I pictured a piece of Mama's soul escaping through her mouth each time she coughed. For how else did Wraiths lose their souls? "Mama!" I ran to her side, wrapping my arms around her midsection as tears burned my eyes.

"Hush, love." Mama stroked my hair. "I'm sorry…'twas only a comment made in bad humor. I have a touch of winter cough. Nothing more."

But the tickle worsened. Her coughs deepened. Mama's face grew paler and gaunter (is this a word? Gaunter?) as fever gripped her bones. Her lungs began emitting a wet, rattling noise when she breathed.

Soon, the cough took a firmer hold. Often, Mama would gag until she spat up a yellow substance she called *mucus*. Toward the end, she choked on blood.

In the final hour of her life, she staggered about our field, plucking tomatoes for The Offering.

I followed her, clutching our well-worn wicker basket, as she lurched between the rows of tomatoes, splattering blood on the Celestial's glistening mesh.

"You'll…be…alright…love." Each word was punctuated by either a wailing wheeze or a rumbling cough. She sluggishly plucked a tomato from the vine, inspected it with bleary eyes, and placed it in the basket. "We'll…finish…and…I need…sleep…"

Blood dribbled down her chin as she bent to retrieve another tomato.

"It's not ripe, Mama," I said. The tomato was green and dull. Not red and shiny as it should have been.

Mama swayed and placed the tomato in the basket. "Remember…love… sunset…don't…tarry…"

She could sense her life drawing to a close.

I could too. My fingers dug into the sharp edges of the basket while sweat pooled beneath my armpits. I began crying long before she collapsed.

And when she finally fell, after collecting only a handful of tomatoes, it was a traumatizing spectacle.

She vomited; spraying blood and bile over the vines, The Offering basket, me, and herself. Her chest made a strange *urk, urk, urk* noise as she struggled to breathe. Her pallid cheeks reddened; a vein pulsed at her temple.

I held her, sobs racking through my body as she suffocated, choking on her own bodily fluids. She toppled backward, bringing me down with her. I laid against her breast, screaming for help. The humans who lived nearby undoubtedly heard my calls, but no one came. The Wraiths, of course, offered no assistance. Why would they? Mama's death meant nothing to them. She was a human, indistinguishable from the rest, and entirely replaceable.

But the event tore my heart to pieces. I couldn't move afterward. My own lungs seemed to have been afflicted with disease as they struggled to bring air into my body. I laid there, curled against Mama's cooling corpse, while the sky above me darkened.

At sunset, the Wraiths came.

IN THE CLEARING, the frog croaked again. *Raaapuh.*

"Mama!" Tears streaked down my cheeks as I stumbled through the bushes. "Mama?"

It wasn't her. And I hadn't truly expected it to be. But when I saw that big, fat toad sitting at the edge of a small pond....

*Raaapuh.*

Rage gripped me. It chased the fear and the cold right out of my body. I'd never experienced such an emotion before, not even when the Wraiths grabbed my hair and tore me away from Mama's body. Not even as I watched those humans cooked over a fire.

But now...

The toad was a portly animal with bulging eyes. It didn't shy away when it saw me. It merely turned and leveled its gaze upon my face. Unafraid. Perhaps it was used to humans and had never been given a reason to fear them. Perhaps it thought me too young, too small, to do any harm.

The scream that burst from my mouth was raw and it clawed painfully at my throat. But I didn't care. I screamed and screamed and screamed. Because there was a hot, uncomfortable sensation curled inside my chest. Like a snake. Coiling and coiling.

My skin itched.

The toad blinked but still didn't move. *Raaapuh.*

"Shut up!" I yelled, clapping my hands over my ears. It drowned out the sounds of the toad, and the nervous twittering of the surrounding animals, but it didn't stop the memories. Over and over, I heard Mama coughing. Over and over, I saw her lifeless eyes staring up at me, her face covered in blood, her chest unnaturally still. I heard the harsh babble of Wraiths as they dragged me to Varn's home, their ~~skelatal~~ —skeletal faces glowing through the darkness while they talked and laughed and jeered at me.

Over and over, I heard my own wails of pain as the Celestial's poisonous blood spread through my veins.

*"Shut up! Shut up! Shut up!"*

A hot, burning itch rippled across my skin. The snake-like sensation coiling inside me was poised, ready to strike.

The toad's bulging eyes were now fearful. Or, as fearful as a toad's eyes were capable of being. But his realization came too late. Before he leapt into the safety of his pond, I caught him.

*"Shut up!"*

The toad was cold and ~~slimey~~ —slimy. I had no intention of hurting him. Truly. I'd only meant to give him a rough shake to quiet him. But it was too late for me as well.

Fire burst from my fingertips, consuming the toad.

I screamed again, this time in fear, and the animal slid from my burning fingertips.

He screeched and writhed as he hit the ground. Flames curled over his body, blistering his ~~slimey~~ —slimy skin. I tried to put them out, but the fire remained wrapped around my fingers, and the more I touched him, the more he burned. In the end, I could do nothing but watch, helpless, as his body gradually stilled, and his cries tapered off.

The fire did not leave my fingertips.

It didn't hurt. Even as flame devoured my hands and singed the sleeves of my tunic, my skin remained unscathed. But I couldn't extinguish it, and everything I touched burned.

"Help!" I flailed my hands through the air, sparks flying from my fingertips. *"Help!"*

But I was alone and too deep into the woods for my pleas to be answered.

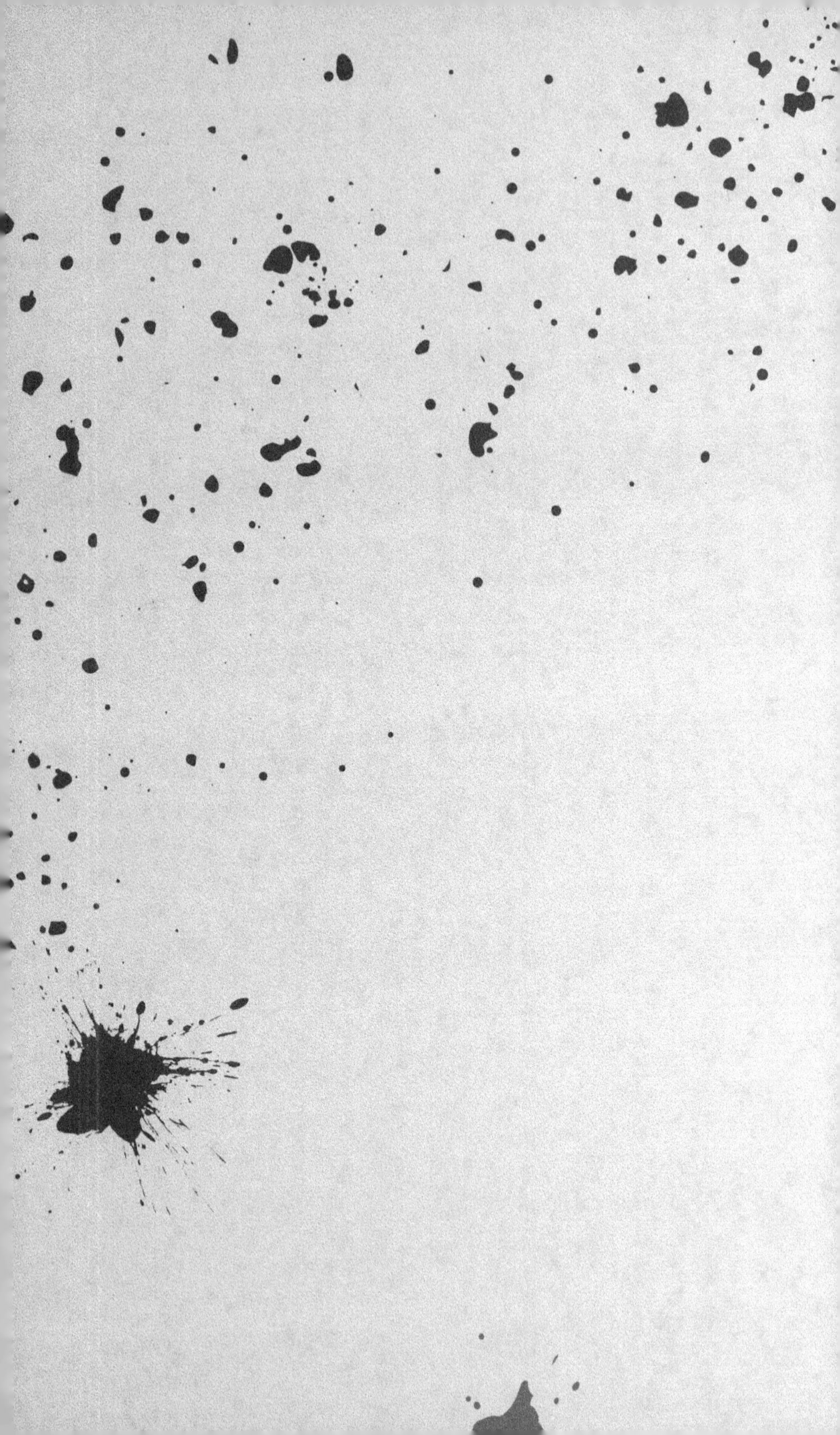

# Terrick

I scorched every blade of grass and destroyed several proud and beautiful trees. The plumes of smoke drove animals from their homes and sent them on a mad scurry to find safety.

"Help!" I screamed until my voice turned coarse. *"Please! Help!"* My fire-wrapped fingers trembled.

The ashy fragrance of smoldering wood and plant life filled the air. Some animals choked or sneezed as they darted through the vapors. It was only after a family of frogs hopped away from me, their eyes bulging, that it occurred to me I was standing near a pond.

"Water is fire's enemy, love," Mama had once said when she'd mended a burn on my palm.

I stepped into the pond, gasping when the cold water bit my skin and plunged my head beneath the surface. It hurt to open my eyes underwater, but I did it anyway, and I blew bubbles when I began crying in relief. The fire was gone!

But it returned once I attempted to step out of the water.

I dove under again. The fire left.

I emerged again. The icy wind lashed across my wet skin, seeming sharp enough to leave wounds.

The fire clung to my flesh, refusing to relinquish its hold.

The cold made my chest tight and sluggish. The water rocked my body, forcing me to shift my feet to maintain my balance…

I screamed when the soft bottom of the pond abruptly vanished, sending me plummeting deep into the water. My arms and legs flailed. Not in an organized fashion, as I didn't know how to swim. These were short, panicked movements, which only made me sink more quickly.

I glanced up, seeing the dim light of the moon shining at the surface. No matter how hard I fought to reach it, the water fought harder to push me down.

Black spots danced before my eyes as my lungs tightened. I reached a hand up, desperately trying to grasp onto something, *anything*, that would help pull me from the water.

I jolted in surprise when my fingers brushed against a soft, yet solid, object.

Another hand.

I was hallucinating, surely.

Fingers wrapped around my wrist. It was a big, powerful hand, and it pulled me to the surface.

The cold air seared my skin and slid like molten metal down my throat.

"It's alright," a voice said in my ear as an arm curled around my shoulder. "Lass…it's alright."

The fire did not return. Perhaps it had fled after being so close to death's embrace. Perhaps it found my waterlogged body a weak host. Regardless, I had vanquished the flame.

And I fainted before my savior carried me to shore.

THE FIRST THING I remembered upon waking was the pain. A band of pressure wrapped around my head. Every time I moved, it tightened. I was sure my skull would buckle. I'd seen enough people die from head injuries to know how horrific it looked. Blood would seep from every ~~orfice~~ orifice: my eyes, nostrils, ears, and mouth. My head would become misshapen, and my face would swell...

"Easy," a voice said as something cold and wet pressed against the back of my neck. A damp scrap of fabric. Oh, it was bliss! The water trickled over my heated skin, cooling me, and easing the pain.

"Try not to move, lass," the voice murmured again. A hand brushed against my shoulder. "This will pass."

And it did, although not immediately.

For several days I drifted in and out of consiousness—conciou—conciousness (I've never fully mastered the spelling of this word). I drifted in and out of *sleep* (I'll use a word I can spell correctly). The pain in my skull refused to abate. It spread, traveling down my neck, across my shoulders, and into my joints. Each time I woke, I cried out, unable to lift my head or open my eyes. And then the voice would speak again in its soft and soothing manner. The damp cloth would drape against the back of my neck, and I'd slip back to sleep.

"'Tis a fever, lass," the voice said on the fourth (or fifth, or perhaps sixth) time I'd awoken. "Rest. Do not fret."

When I next crawled out of the murky depths of sleep, my eyelids felt as heavy as stones. The dim light of the morning sun drove scalding needles into my head. Tears blurred my vision, and nausea clawed at my stomach, but I kept my eyes open.

A figure moved toward me, but I couldn't make out his features until he knelt on the ground beside me. It was a man —a *human* man.

"Easy," the man said when I tried to sit up. "Easy." He had a deep, rumbling voice.

It reminded me of a boy in Detha who had once lived a few dwellings away from Mama's. He'd been little more than a child, but his booming voice had sounded decades older. Conn, his name had been. He'd always been so gentle, so kind, especially to the younger children.

He'd died before he reached adulthood.

But the man who knelt before me now…

"You're so *old!*" I blurted.

In Detha, people seldom made it to adulthood. Those that did often didn't survive *long* into adulthood.

So it was quite a shock to see a man this old: his dark skin crinkled with age, his hair stark white.

The man chuckled. The wrinkles around his eyes deepened when he smiled. "I suppose I am, yes," he said. "To your eyes, I must seem ancient."

I watched his gnarled hands as he wrung water from a piece of fabric. "Who are you?" I asked.

"My name is Terrick." He pressed the cool cloth to the back of my neck. "And it's nice to see you awake. You were firmly in the fever's grip. I—you," he sighed. "Do you remember what happened? At the pond?"

I did. But I said nothing.

"Were you trying to start a fire, lass?"

I remained silent.

"You may have been too close to the bushes. That's why you lost control over it. But fortune was with you that night. Had I not seen the smoke, I wouldn't have been able to save you."

So he didn't know. He thought I'd been trying to kindle wood. He hadn't seen the fire erupting from my skin.

I didn't know whether I was relieved or disappointed by this revelation.

"I can show you how to safely start a fire, if you'd like." Terrick pressed a hand to my shoulder. His palm was massive; he could have wrapped his fingers twice around the thickest part of my arm.

And it was only when he touched me that I realized how shaken I'd become.

The tremors ran along my spine, aggravating the ache in my skull. I whimpered and squeezed my eyes shut.

"It's alright," Terrick pulled the blanket tighter around me. I hadn't even realized he'd given me a blanket. He'd also given me fabric to pillow my head and had laid me in a small stone cave, where I was shielded from the worst of the elements. He'd taken care of me.

"What's your name, lass?" Terrick asked.

I opened my mouth to respond, but I couldn't remember.

No matter how many times I combed through my memories, I couldn't recall my name. Mama had hardly used it, preferring to call me *love* or *darling*.

But others had used my name, hadn't they?

Why couldn't I remember?

"It's alright." Terrick wrapped his warm fingers around my trembling knuckles. "Perhaps it will come to you later."

I shook harder. I didn't like this man; didn't like how big his hands were, how he seemed to tower over me, how solidly he was built. I was accustomed to the people of Detha, who'd often been little more than walking ~~skeltons~~ skeletons. And I wanted…

"Mama," I whispered.

Terrick's weathered face drooped. "I don't know where your mother is," he whispered. "Do you remember where you saw her last?"

In our field, her lifeless eyes gazing at the sky. Her skin growing cold—not immediately, of course. But I'd sat by her side for hours, praying she'd wake up. "'Tis but a cough, darling," she'd told me when she first became ill. Her hands, even then, were icy as she stroked my cheeks. "I will not allow it to be stronger than me. Besides, I have you, don't I?" She smiled, although it was ~~tremorless~~ tremulous and didn't reach her eyes. "Your love will keep me alive."

But she hadn't been stronger than the cough. And my love was worthless because it hadn't stopped her from dying.

"Easy." Terrick's massive hands reached behind me, pulling me into a sitting position.

Tears slid down my cheeks.

"It's alright," Terrick's bear-like arms pulled me against him, pressing my face into the solid slope of his shoulder. "You're safe, lass," he murmured. "You're safe."

He held me as though I were made of glass and he feared I would shatter. But his kindness, his gentleness, and his soothing voice only strengthened my sobs.

I cried until my chest and stomach hurt. Until it seemed as though I had expended all the fluid in my body. I cried until my eyes were swollen and a sticky feeling coated my tongue. All the while, Terrick held me, his body warm, his arms encircling me. Protecting me.

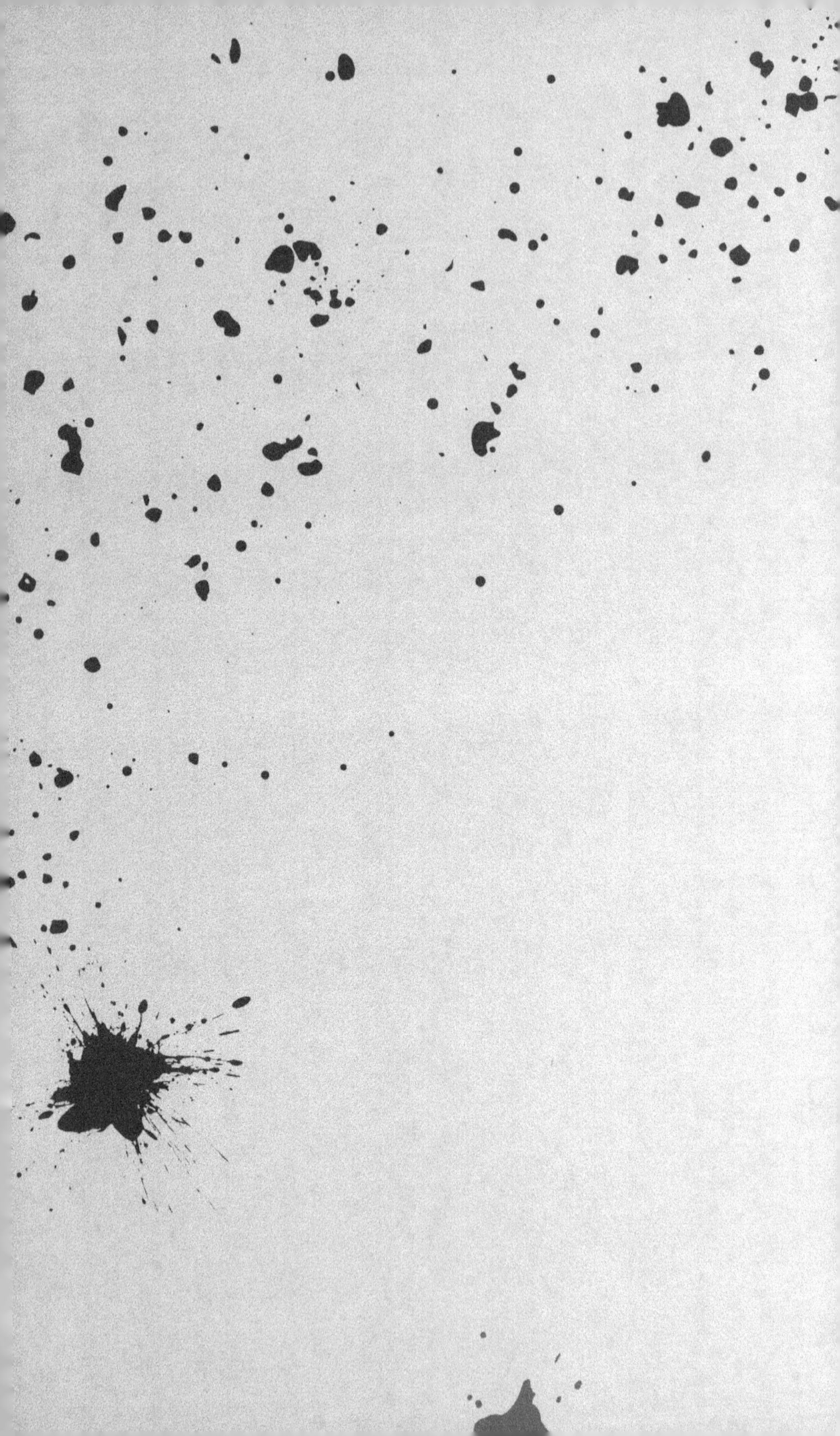

# Mutiny

Terrick, as it turned out, was…

"A hybrid," he said.

"There's no such thing," I sniffed. The boy from Detha, Conn, had told us stories about them. Hybrids. Humans given Celestial powers. But Conn was *always* telling stories. Mama used to say he had ears sharper than a two-edged sword.

"That boy misses *nothing*," she would groan whenever I'd repeat one of his tales. "Don't mind what he says, love. He ~~eggaerates~~ exaggerates."

"And yet, I *am* a hybrid." Terrick winked and plucked a stone off the ground. "Watch." He stretched his arm out, cupping the stone in the palm of his hand. It was a small rock, caked with dirt.

And then it vanished.

I gasped, reaching for his hand.

The stone was still there. I felt its jagged edges when I traced my fingers along Terrick's palm, but I could not *see* it.

"I'm a Concealer." Terrick fluttered his fingers, and the rock reappeared.

I took the stone from him, pressing it against my nose to inspect every crevice and flake of dirt on its surface. "You've tricked me. Somehow," I accused.

Terrick laughed. "I have not. It's my ability. To Conceal; to make objects, or people, seem like they've vanished, even when they're still in front of us. Here…" He grasped my hand and pressed it to the ground.

My fingers disappeared before my very eyes. They were still there, of course, but they'd adapted the same color and stringy texture as the brown grass. When I shifted my hand to grasp the stone, my skin changed again, this time appearing as gray and coarse as the rock.

I touched my other finger to the back of my Concealed hand. My skin remained smooth and pliant, despite looking jagged and rigid.

All the while, Terrick kept a light hold on my wrist. His fingers grew cold and sweat-slick as I poked, prodded, and marveled at my Concealed flesh. Once he let go, my hand returned to its normal shape and color.

I stared at him, excitement simmering in my chest. "Can you Conceal the bush next? Or the tree?" I pointed to a thin pine.

Terrick laughed, even as he wiped a trickle of sweat from his brow. "No, lass. My abilities are not so powerful. And not nearly as ostentatious as what other hybrids can do. Especially the Illuminators! They are quite a marvel to behold. Aiden is an Illuminator—he is my neighbor. Well, it has been a few years since I left Swindon, so I *hope* he is still my neighbor."

I swallowed. This wasn't the first time Terrick had mentioned this place. *Swindon.* He'd been journeying there when he found me.

"You're recovering your strength quickly now. And

you've kept your meals down for the second day." Terrick's palm rested upon my shoulder.

I had, indeed, successfully consumed three small meals of berries and dried meats, after days of fighting with a ~~rebelus~~ —rebellious stomach that had rejected everything I ate. This was a good thing, Terrick kept telling me. It meant the last of the fever had left my body.

But now my stomach began churning again.

"I'd imagine you'll be well enough to travel in a few days," Terrick continued. "You'll *adore* Swindon, lass. There are no Wraiths there…"

A Wraith-free city.

Conn had spoken of this notion before. Only once. And his words had come with dire consequences.

"THERE ARE Celestials on our side. Not many, mind. But enough. And humans once fought beside 'em, they did." Conn's hands flew through the air as he recited his tale. It was dusk, and adults often sent small children away from their dwellings while The Offering was prepared. Conn was always eager to keep us entertained. He'd seen us gathered in the alleyway between the rows of dwellings and had sat on the cold, muddy ground beside us. As Conn was only a few years away from adulthood, he looked abnormally long and gangly as he hunched in that dark alley with us young ones.

"'Twas a land not far from here. The humans there said, 'we don't want to serve the Celestials.'" Conn swiped a hand through his gnarled brown hair as he continued. He was too exuberant to be still. "And the Celestials—the good 'uns—

they said 'help us win and you'll get your wish.' So the humans—they weren't much for fighting, mind—they made their own weapons and stood beside the Celestials. 'Tis said Ramiel 'imself was there…"

A few children squealed in fright. I stayed silent, only because my heart seemed to have taken residence in my throat.

It was a name we knew well. Ramiel. The Conqueror. The Celestial we all feared the most.

"Ah, but 'e did not have a mind to attack the humans," Conn chuckled at our terrified faces. "'Twas his brethren he wished to fight. So the Celestials fought each other, and the humans fought the Wraiths—ah yes," he whispered when another murmur of fear traveled around the group. "They fought *Wraiths*. They were brave souls, them humans. Many lives were lost. But the humans won. And they was given the freedom they asked for. Never again will Wraiths haunt those lands. Never again will humans go hungry while Celestials feast on their crops. They are *free*." He became breathless, his dark eyes glistening with excitement. And, naturally, he'd gotten the children tittering (this is a word, is it not?) with ~~exhileration~~ *exhilaration* as well.

We loved Conn's stories.

But such tales were not permitted in Detha.

Two days later, Conn was whipped until his back was torn and bloodied.

Open wounds became angry wounds if not tended properly, Mama always said. Angry wounds led to fever.

Conn's wounds became angry.

The last time I saw him, he staggered through the alleyway where the children gathered at dusk. His normally sun-kissed face was whiter than a fresh sheet of snow. Sweat dripped from his brow, despite the winter's chill. His fever-bright eyes were focused on something in the distance. He did not stop. We called out to him, but he ignored us.

Death visited him that night.

A week later, a group of boys—Conn's friends—mutinied.

Ice coated the ground that morning. I slid on it as I stepped outside our dwelling.

"Careful, love." Mama grasped my arm as a wet cough bubbled inside her.

Above us sat a heavy, gray sky. Something cold slithered inside my gut, although it was not caused by the dull, early morning light.

Dread. Mama had always called that sensation *dread*.

She seemed to feel it too. Her fingers trembled around my arm.

"Mama—" I started.

"Hush," she hissed.

The boys emerged from the alley, armed with sharp slabs of wood. A few had strapped pieces of tree bark to their torsos, an attempt to mimic the Wraiths' armor.

Mama's breath shuddered as the boys crossed the street, gathering by Conn's dwelling.

Other families emerged from their dwellings. Some returned indoors when they caught sight of the boys. Most carried on with their chores but cast worried glances at the cluster.

A few brightened at the prospect of a mutiny.

"Ah," a rosy-cheeked woman exclaimed. She placed her hands on her hips, surveying the boys. "And you'll think you'll kill Wraiths with them stakes, eh?"

One boy, the tallest in the group, clutched onto his shard of wood so tightly, his knuckles whitened. "No. But we'll all be dyin' soon anyway, so why not try? It's what Conn would've wanted."

The rosy-cheeked woman nodded grimly. "Agreed." She

returned to her dwelling but re-emerged a moment later wielding a broad piece of firewood. "And I'll be joinin' ya. I'm getting too bloody old to be making bread for those ungrateful sods. These hands aren't what they used to be, but they've got some strength left."

Others joined. Soon the group of mutineers boasted almost two dozen members.

Mama's hand never stopped trembling. She did not move to begin her chores. Nor did she join the mutineers. She simply stood still, her lips drawn into a tight line. "Inside," she whispered to me.

Her head whipped to the side when Wraiths marched down the street. Their black armor glinted in the gray light.

The mutineers, now trembling, brandished their wooden weapons. "We'll not be workin' today," the tallest boy yelled.

"You tell the Celestials they can make their own bloody bread," the rosy-cheeked woman spat.

"We work this land," a broad man said. "We tend the animals. This is *our* city."

"Inside. Now!" Mama shoved me through the door, ignoring my protests.

"Mama!" The inside of our dwelling was dark and quiet. The slippery sensation inside me grew, threatening to crawl up my throat. I dug my nails into the closed door, wanting, *needing*, to be back outside with Mama.

"Stay there, love." Mama's voice quivered. "Don't come out. No matter what you hear."

I never asked why Mama remained outside. Likely she feared she would be seen as a mutineer if she failed to begin her chores, but she wished to shield me from the bloodshed. I saw it anyway.

Through the narrow wooden slats of our door, I watched as the group of mutineers attacked.

The humans were ill-equipped and too weak to battle the

Wraiths. The minutes-long ordeal turned into a ~~massacer~~ massacre.

Afterward, half of the ~~rebelus~~ rebellious humans were taken alive, and screaming, to Varn's house. The rest were left to die on the street.

We were not permitted to tend their wounds, give them water, or ease their suffering. Instead, the Wraiths gathered us in a half circle around the mangled bodies and forced us to watch as they gasped their final breaths.

But that was not the last time I saw the mutineers.

The rosy-cheeked woman found me on the day Mama died.

Her skin had turned gray, her cheeks hollow. Her white eyes roamed apathetically (this is spelled correctly, is it not?) over me as I cowered by Mama's body. She was a mere shadow of the woman she'd once been. But I recognized her voice as she cited my crime: failing to prepare The Offering.

The woman ignored my frightened wails and shrill pleas as she took me to Varn. There was no compassion or sorrow left in her. How could there be? She no longer had a soul.

She'd been amongst the group taken to Varn's house on the day of the mutiny. And they had turned her into the very thing she'd sought to destroy: a Wraith.

Some fates were far worse than death.

"Lass?"

I startled as Terrick clasped a weathered hand to my shoulder. "You've gone pale."

I turned away, tears burning my eyes.

"We can wait if you'd like," he said. "I've plenty of food

and supplies still. Winter is leaving us. We need not go to Swindon right away. We can wait until you're ready."

I wouldn't *ever* be ready.

I'd seen what happened when humans tried to break free of Wraiths, and I didn't want to know what atrocities awaited me at Swindon.

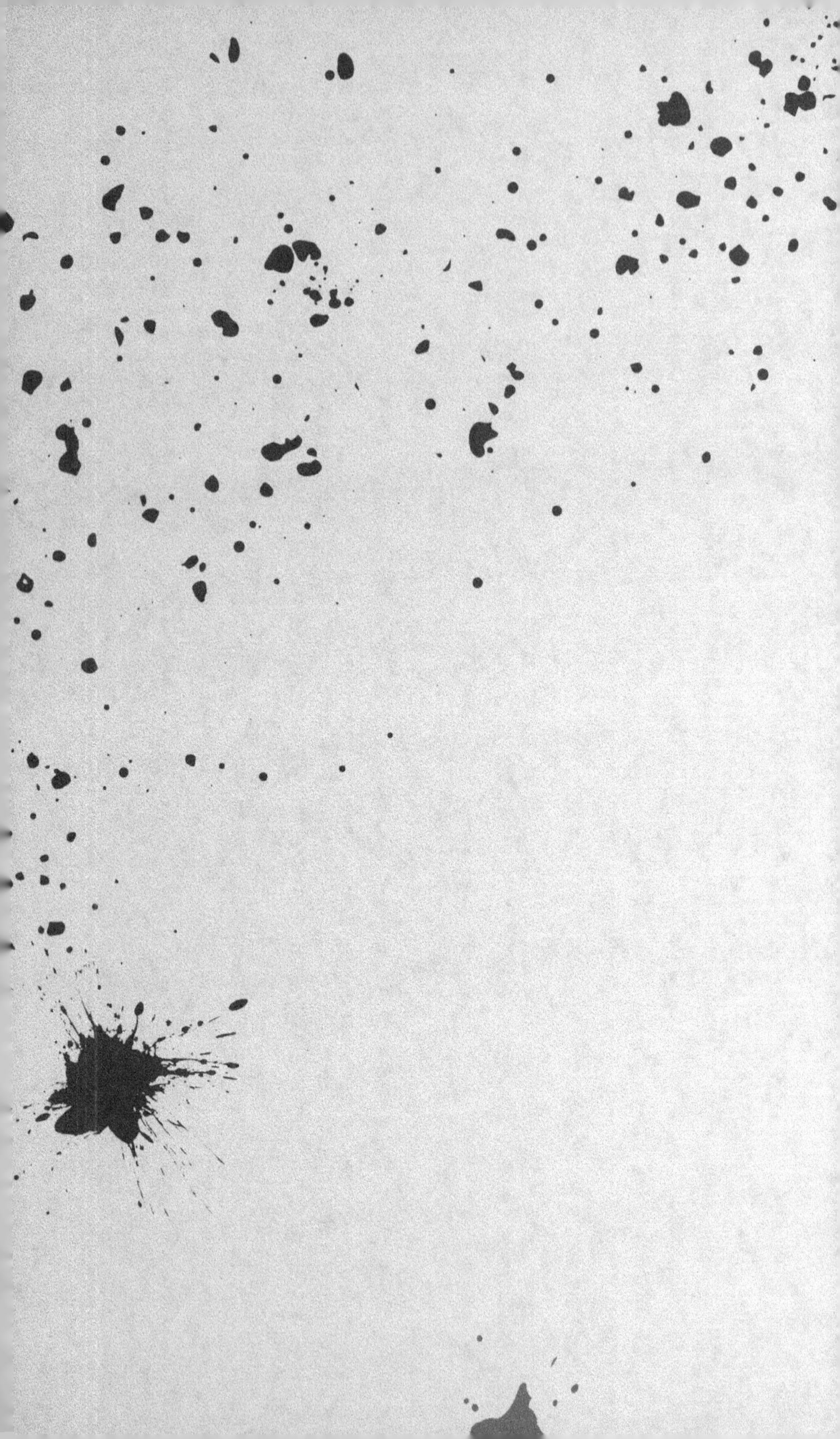

# Swindon

Terrick and I emerged from the forest on a late-summer afternoon.

I'd spent much of the morning ailing with an aching belly, so Terrick carried me through the last leg of our journey. I clutched at his neck with slick, trembling hands, and buried my face into his shoulder. Terrick always smelled like pine needles. The scent had become a comfort.

"There now, lass," he murmured as we approached the town called Swindon. "I'm putting you down."

"No!" I clung to him.

"Yes. You're perfectly capable of walking." He bent, depositing my feet onto the ground. "Now…open your eyes, lass." His rough, gnarled hand touched my cheek.

"I can't. They're stuck." I raised my chin.

Terrick tapped my shoulder. "Don't lie."

I drew back when he grasped my hand. "I won't go!"

"We're already here."

"I hate Wraiths! *Hate* them! I want to go back to the woods."

"There are no Wraiths in Swindon."

"*'Don't lie,'*" I repeated his earlier statement.

"Lass." Laughter warmed Terrick's voice. "I'll strike a bargain with you. If you open your eyes and see a Wraith, we'll return to the woods. If you cannot find one, then you'll accompany me into Swindon. Does that sound fair?"

It did, but I said nothing.

I pried my eyelids apart and angled my head toward the village. I expected to see ramshackled (is this a word?) dwellings and armored Wraiths.

Instead, rows upon rows of houses lined the village streets. Some buildings were as big as Varn's home. Most were bigger. Humans walked to and fro—and they were unlike any humans I'd ever seen. They were so very *large*. And robust. Layers of fat and muscle covered their bones. They wore hole-less clothes.

(This doesn't seem right. Whole-less? Holeless? Not holey?)

Well, in Detha, our threadbare clothing had provided little warmth or protection. And, when the fabric wore through, there often wasn't any spare cloth to patch the holes. But in Swindon, the humans wore thick cloth; their tunics and breeches unmarred by tears. And *boots!* Only a dozen humans in Detha had possessed a pair of boots. Everyone had a pair in Swindon!

"Have you found a Wraith?" Terrick asked.

My eyes roamed over every building, human, and animal I could find. There were no Wraiths.

Still, I said nothing—I never did like admitting when I was wrong—as I followed Terrick into the town.

"That's the shoemaker." Terrick pointed to a small, triangular building with a wooden sign in the shape of a boot hanging over the front door. "We can go there in the morning to have shoes made for you. And here—" Terrick nodded toward a small, paunchy building. "Millie, the seamstress, will make you proper clothing. She's the only one in the village with *colored* fabrics. You could have a green tunic if you wish. Or *blue*.

"And Carragh…" Terrick's voice lowered as we passed a portly old woman selling bread from a wooden stand. I looked at him and found his cheeks tinged pink. "She is the finest bread maker in Swindon. Perhaps in all of Sakar." A smile stretched across his lips. Despite his praise, he barely spared her steaming loaves of bread a glance. Instead, he kept his eyes focused on her, only drawing his gaze back to me once we turned a corner. "What do you think so far, lass?"

Truthfully, I was stunned. And my neck ached. This lively, noisy, *wondrous* place had me twisting in every direction, trying to absorb all the new sights, sounds, and smells. I wished I had more than two eyes. Or that I could turn my head all the way around. Like an owl.

The scent of cooked meat drifted through the air as we passed the market. My stomach gave a hungry grumble.

Terrick chuckled. "There will be food at the inn, lass," he assured me.

"In?"

"Yes. A tavern. Temporary housing," he amended when I furrowed my brow. "My home is likely unlivable at the moment. It's been years since I've…well, we'll be far more comfortable at the inn."

As we moved toward the heart of the town, the other humans began to notice us. Slowly, at first. A few odd glances here and there. The occasional raised eyebrow. Many of them recognized Terrick. They called out to him. He waved cheerily back. Sometimes they made jests at his expense.

"Oi, Terrick," a man said, "where did you find that wee little thing?"

"A child? At your age?" another man asked with a hearty chuckle. "My, my Terrick. I've misjudged you."

"I have always been full of surprises, Jethro," Terrick laughed, even as he gave my arm a gentle squeeze.

"Ah, such a sweet lass," a stooped, toothless woman said when we passed by her. She pinched my cheek and laid her hand on Terrick's arm. "It's good to see you again, Terrick. You look happy."

We walked. And we walked. And we walked. The streets seemed never-ending, the people too numerous to count. They were boisterous; full of life and joy. They ate and drank freely. Laughed loudly. Some played music. Some sang.

In Detha, they would have all been whipped for causing such a ruckus.

In Swindon, it seemed there were no such rules. But still my eyes roamed, endlessly shifting through the masses of humans.

"Have you seen a Wraith, Lass?" Terrick asked as we passed a tavern. Screeching music drifted through the doors while scores of men and women slurred and sang in horribly off-key tones.

Heat spread through my chest. Embarrassment. "No." It pained me to admit defeat.

Terrick's weathered face wrinkled as he smiled.

TERRICK RENTED a room for a month at *The Black Bull Inn*; so named because of the innkeeper's bull. The ~~behometh~~ behemoth creature was prime breeding stock with his lusty, rippling muscles and shining black fur. He seemed terrifying; almost too large to be a real animal. But he was as mild as a kitten. And I adored him. I spent many a morning perched on the top railing of his pen, sharing my porridge. I ate a spoonful, fed him a spoonful, and so on until my bowl emptied. Afterward, I traced my fingers around the swirl of hair on the bull's brow while he leaned his massive head against my lap, utterly content.

The innkeeper, Lorcan, was the bull's human counterpart: a thickly muscled man with a scarred face and a kind heart. He called me *cailín álainn* — or *pretty girl*.

"Ah, *cailín álainn!*" he greeted me in the mornings. "I've added some berries for you." He winked as he handed me the bowl of porridge. "But let's keep that secret between us, shall we? I don't want my other patrons to be jealous. And be sure Noro doesn't take more than his share."

Noro, of course, being the black bull.

At first, Noro consumed most of the berries. Truthfully, I was stricken with terror at the thought of eating the fruits; a delicacy I'd never been permitted to indulge in. Surely it would have been more beneficial for the delectable little treats to go to Lorcan's prized bull?

But Lorcan added a handful of the sweet fruit to my porridge every morning and, eventually, the temptation became too great. I ate one. Two. They were ~~equistite~~ (that's certainly not the correct spelling. ~~Eqsuite?~~ *Exquisite?):* bitter, yet sweeter than even Mama's finest tomatoes. And, well, Noro seemed content with the porridge, so I kept the berries for myself.

Those first days were simple. Quiet. Terrick woke at dawn and went to complete the renovations to his dwelling.

"It's fallen into disrepair," he told me. "But it's nothing I can't fix. You'll love it there, lass. Our lodgings are above the shop. Although not quite as big as what we have here at the inn," he gestured to the spacious room we were renting, "it will be all ours. There's even a livery barn. Perhaps I'll find a bull for you to keep there." He smiled when I gasped in excitement.

While Terrick was away, I played with Noro or helped Lorcan clean the tables in the tavern. Or, sometimes, I rested in our rented room, curled against the windowsill, watching the busy village life below. I was usually sad on those days. Sad that Mama, Conn, and all the people from Detha would never know a vibrant life such as this.

But the sad days became fewer as the weeks passed. 'Tis the ~~resilency~~ resiliency of a child, I suppose. I'd been too young to hold on to dark emotions. Too young to dwell on the past when my future looked so bright.

And when Terrick deemed his dwelling livable again, I was given an important task: to help him reopen his shop.

His *book* shop.

It's a rather silly notion. Terrick earned coin by selling parchment bound in scraps of leather. He called them fiction books. Meaning that, while the stories seemed real, and sometimes frightening, they weren't. There was nothing historical or factual about them. They were the product of someone's imagination.

As I said, it's a silly notion. Why would someone wish to waste ink and parchment on a *lie*?

But, in Swindon, the townspeople adored Terrick's fiction books. They celebrated when he reopened his shop.

"Ten years, Terrick," one woman cried. "You've made me wait *ten years* to discover what happened to the boy wizard!"

"Apologies, Róise," Terrick bowed his head as he handed the woman a broad tome. "But after…well, the time away has done me good." He turned to where I was dusting his fiction books and gave me a playful wink.

There was darkness in Terrick's past, although I never asked him about it. At the time, I hadn't noticed it, even though the evidence was there.

For instance, a great armoire occupied much of the wall space in our dwelling. I passed it every day. Sometimes I amused myself by tracing my fingers over the intricately designed flowers carved into the wood, or marveling at the gowns inside. And I never questioned why Terrick possessed an armoire full of lady's clothes.

Terrick gifted me with trinkets when we moved into his dwelling. Toys, he'd called them. Wooden figurines of horses, and other objects. ~~Frivoulous~~ frivolous things, clearly made for small hands. Like mine. They were already old and well-used when I received them. I lovingly played with them every day but never asked where they came from.

During those early months at Swindon, I busied myself with my ~~indulgances~~ indulgences: eating until my stomach felt as though it would burst. Proudly polishing my new boots and telling another girl that I had the *finest* boots in town. She, of course, maintained her boots were finer, while her brother was convinced *he* possessed the superior boots. Our shoes were identical (quite like the girl and her brother). They'd been crafted at the same shop, likely with the same strip of cowhide. But we did rather enjoy teasing each other.

Terrick, sadly, couldn't find a bull, but he brought goats into the livery barn. Wee bastards. They ate everything: my food, my clothes, Terrick's fiction books. One even tried to gnaw on the toe of my precious boots.

I *adored* the little buggards.

They were warm, and soft, and had tolerant dispositions. They didn't care if I sang while I cleaned their pens—I was, and still am, a wretched singer. I'm certain the dulcet tones of my voice damaged their hearing. They didn't bite or kick when I played with them, which often involved me hanging onto their necks, fiddling with their ears, and kissing their noses. And they stood patiently while Terrick taught me how to coax milk from their udders.

I still remember the day Terrick gave me my first cup of the creamy liquid.

"It's good for you," Terrick laughed as I savored the thick concoction. "Some people believe it helps children grow."

"Helps them how?" I asked.

"It makes your bones strong."

"How?"

Terrick smiled. "It coats them, like armor, and protects them from injury while you grow."

"Ah." And, considering I was the smallest, and thinnest child in my age group, I diligently drank the goat's milk every morning. Sadly, Terrick was wrong in his belief. I grew. All children do. But I remain, to this day, smaller than most.

All in all, we lived in that splendid town for over six years. The Golden Days, as I've always called them. Where happiness reigned and darkness seemed like a distant memory.

Of course, it was not us who decided to leave Swindon.

We were chased out of the town.

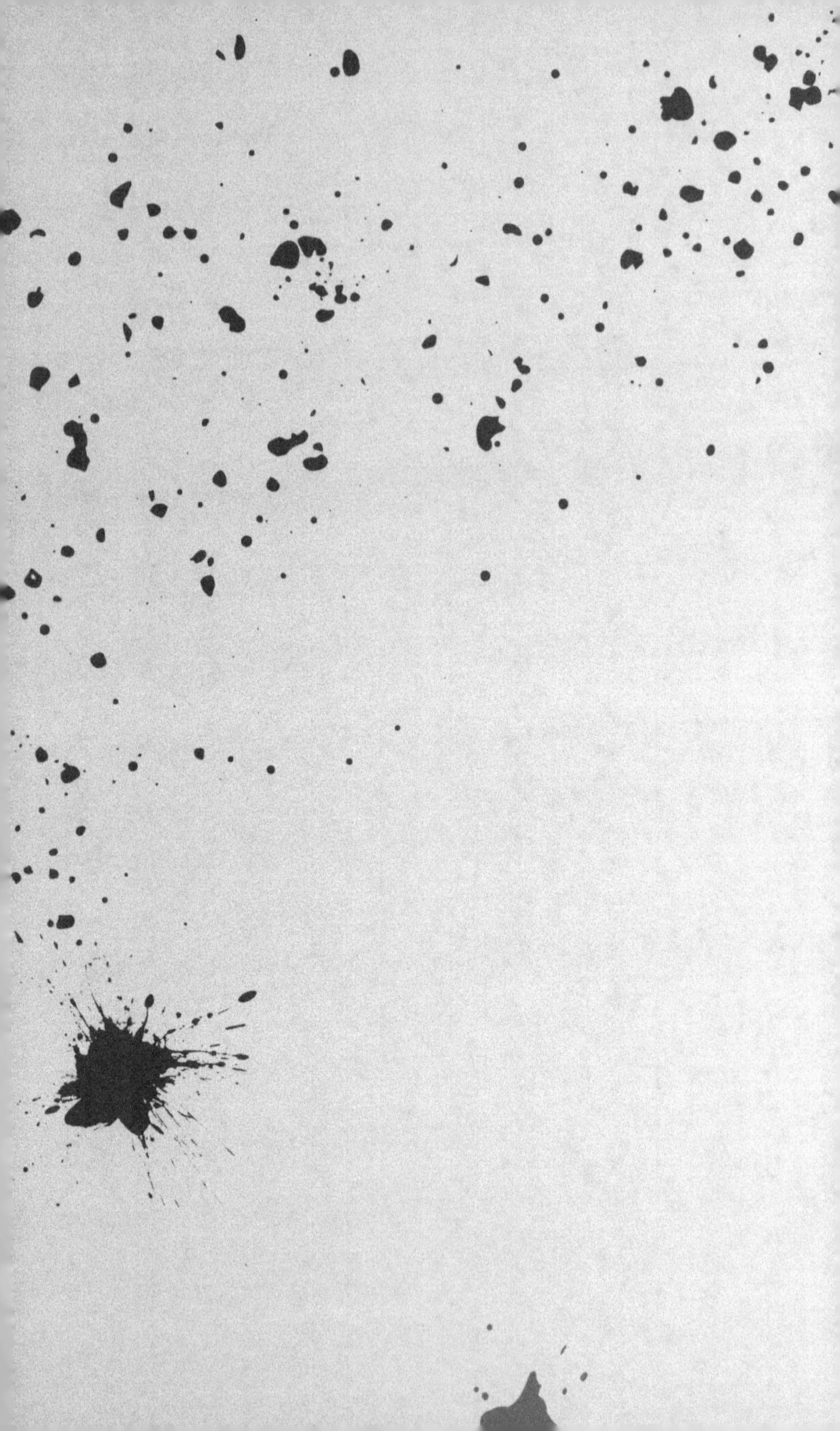

# The Incident

Humans are flawed creatures. We are more intelligent than other beasts of the earth; capable of great kindness, empathy, and creativity. Yet many of us are ruled by the same base emotions that drive a boar to attack, or a hound to hunt. For all our advancements and so-called intelligence, we are little better than animals.

My first experience with cruelty—*human* cruelty—came after we'd lived in Swindon for over six years.

THE...*INCIDENT* occurred on a tranquil winter evening.

The market had begun to close for the night, but Terrick had sent me to retrieve a loaf of bread to have with supper. He had an insatiable appetite for bread.

And for the bread maker.

"Ach, you're a lucky girl," Carragh told me as she handed me her last loaf. "I was about to give this to the pigs. It won't be much good tomorrow—likely'll be harder than a rock. You and Terrick best eat it tonight."

"We will." I tucked the bread under my arm and handed her a coin.

She waved my hand away. "No, child. I'll not be takin' payment for stale bread."

"If you do not take it now, Terrick will bring it later." I smiled at the hopeful expression that crossed her face.

I may have been young, but I was not foolish. Carragh and Terrick enjoyed each other's company.

"Keep your coin." Carragh fought to keep from smiling.

"As you wish." I turned and walked back through the market, jiggling the coin in my hand. Many of the vendors had retired for the evening. Indeed, when I turned a corner, I found the street deserted, and the booths emptied.

Except one. The dressmaker, Darcie.

I liked Darcie. She was kind, and never without a smile. She hadn't even gotten angry when my buck, Ned, had escaped his pen the year before and gleefully explored the market, consuming everything in his path. Including one of Darcie's fine gowns.

Darcie had merely laughed as I'd wrestled the cloth from Ned's tightly clamped jaw. She'd also refused Terrick's payment, claiming the entertainment she'd received watching me corral my wayward goat had been fair compensation for the gown.

Normally, Darcie would have packed her fabrics away before sunset. But, that night, they still hung from the booth, flapping in the breeze.

The sight was unusual, but not a cause for concern. Until I heard the cry. It was muffled and quiet, but unmistakably afraid. Most children might have run away from the noise; perhaps to fetch an adult. It's what I should've done. Instead,

I foolishly ran *toward* the sound, batting the fluttering dresses away as I peered over the booth.

Darcie lay face-down on the ground. She'd been stripped of her clothing.

A man crouched over her. I recognized him, but only vaguely. Grady, I believe his name was. He was a market vendor as well, but one Terrick had rarely visited.

Grady was still clothed but had pulled his trousers to his knees. His reddened face was contorted in what looked to be pain. One gnarled hand clasped over Darcie's mouth, the other yanked on a fistful of her hair.

At the time, I didn't fully comprehend what I was seeing. I was too young. I'd never seen humans copulating before. But I still knew something was wrong.

I backed away, a cold sensation writhing along my spine. The loaf of bread slipped from my numb fingers, landing on the booth with a loud thud.

Darcie whipped her head up.

A steady stream of blood ran from her nose. Grady had struck her. Likely several times. Bruises marred her throat and shoulders. Her wild, terrified eyes found mine.

She tried to speak—perhaps to ask for help. But with Grady's palm stuffed between her lips, all that came out was a stifled gag.

*Raaaphuh.*

My skin prickled.

Before me, Darcie roiled in pain against the ground. But, in my memories, I saw Mama collapsing in the tomato field. I saw that great big toad, with his bulging eyes.

My blood coursed like fire through my veins. My palms itched.

I wanted to help Darcie. But my emotions whirled in a dizzying frenzy and my body seemed to have turned to stone. I couldn't move toward her. Nor could I step away.

*Raaaphuh,* came Darcie's muffled plea.

"Stop," I whispered, clasping my hands over my ears. It dulled the noise but did nothing to ease the raging itch spreading across my skin.

Grady drew back. "Oi!" he bellowed.

Darcie tried to yell. *Haapufh!*

"Stop! Stop!" I closed my eyes and screamed.

I don't remember what happened next. Perhaps my brain rid itself of the traumatic memory. I'm told that is possible; the human brain is quite fascinating.

Regardless, the next thing I knew, I stood before the smoldering market booth, staring in horror at the two bodies on the ground. Both Grady and Darcie were unrecognizable—their flesh turned mottled shades of black and red. Their faces were swollen and puffy, teeth bared as though in agony.

They weren't breathing.

"No, no, no," I whispered.

Flames danced over my fingertips.

Another scream filled the air, but this one was not from Darcie.

Darcie would never scream again.

Instead, Carragh stood a short distance away. One hand covered her mouth, the other was outstretched, her trembling finger pointing at me. "You-you…*what have you done?*"

I stared at her, a chill gripping my body despite the fire that frolicked over my skin. The scent of charred flesh filled my nostrils.

More people spilled onto the street.

"A hybrid?" Some questioned as they studied me.

"Impossible," others scoffed. "No hybrid has that ability."

"That's Seruf's power. Mark my words."

~~Consternation~~ Consternation filled their eyes as they circled me. Some faces I recognized. Lorcan, for example. The innkeeper who'd once put berries in my porridge.

"Help," I whimpered. "Help!"

The fire would not abate. It traveled along my arms. The sleeves of my fine green tunic were reduced to ash.

My skin remained unblemished.

"Help me!" I whirled in panic. Embers floated from my body. They looked like stars against the night sky.

"She'll burn the market down!" A man said.

Tears filled my eyes when people began drawing weapons.

"Please!" I gasped.

Lorcan stepped forward.

"Please *help me!*" I staggered to his side.

He whispered, "I'm sorry, *cailín álainn,*" before he struck my head with the blunt end of a knife.

I awoke back in Terrick's dwelling.

"Lass." He knelt beside my bed, pressing a damp cloth to my brow.

"Don't touch me!" I sprang up, staring at my fingers.

But the fire was gone.

"It's alright, lass," Terrick whispered. His gnarled hands shook as he wrapped them around my knuckles. "Lorcan said the flames disappeared once you were ~~unconcious~~ unconscious. It's alright. Oh, lass…"

A long wail burst from my throat. It *hurt*, as though Lorcan had speared his knife through my chest.

Terrick pulled me into a tight embrace, rocking me slowly back and forth as I howled and quivered. He dried my tears, pressed cool cloths to my neck, and guarded me when I slipped into an uneasy slumber.

It was a night that would haunt me for the rest of my life. Even to this day, I see Darcie and Grady when I close my eyes. I smell their burnt flesh in my dreams.

They were the first humans to be destroyed by my wretched power.

But they would not be the last.

TERRICK MUST HAVE BEEN TERROR-STRICKEN. I was a hybrid that shouldn't have existed. One with the same power as the Firestarter Celestial: Seruf, Ramiel's trusted companion.

And I had no control over my ability. I was volatile. Dangerous. Had Terrick decided to abandon me, he would have been justified in doing so. I was not his kin. I was merely a girl he'd found in the woods.

But he stayed by my side, assuring me I was not to blame for what had happened.

Meanwhile, the people of Swindon, the kind-hearted folk we'd lived alongside for six years, turned on us.

Accusations swirled around the village:

"You never said she was a hybrid, Terrick!"

"Is she *truly* a hybrid? I've never heard of one with such a destructive ability."

"She couldn't control it."

"She killed two people!"

"How do we know Seruf didn't create her? Has she, perhaps, been Seruf's spy all along?"

"She'll kill again. Mark my words."

Terrick tried to plead my innocence. "The lass stumbled across a traumatic event. And, for a child to see such a thing…but it doesn't mean she *can't* control her powers. You know her! She's a good lass. She won't hurt anyone else."

His words fell upon deaf ears.

The townspeople, long frightened by the Celestials' wrath, would never trust me.

People stopped visiting his shop. They kept a distance

when we walked through the streets. Eventually, vendors found excuses to withhold their merchandise from Terrick.

"I've got no eggs today, Terrick. The hens are old—don't produce as much as they used to." The rather rotund man wouldn't even look at us.

"Ah, yes, but I'm afraid the last pig is already spoken for. Perhaps if you'd arrived sooner?" The pig keeper rubbed a hand against the back of her neck and turned away.

The most hurtful betrayal was Lorcan's. When Terrick and I approached the inn, hoping for a hot meal, Lorcan waved a knife at me. "I'll not have you coming near this place anymore, girl," he said.

*Girl.*

I was *cailín álainn* no more,

And Swindon no longer welcomed me.

It still could've been a safe haven for Terrick. All he had to do was rid himself of me. But he didn't.

"I'll never leave you, Lass," he told me on one of the many nights I cried myself to sleep. He pressed his lips to my brow, holding me close while sobs wracked my body. "You are not evil. Nor are you a monster. The townspeople are frightened. They've seen too many horrors in their lives. Do not listen to them."

So, we prepared to leave our home.

And what the townspeople never knew, or perhaps never understood, was that they could never fear or hate me as much as I feared and hated myself.

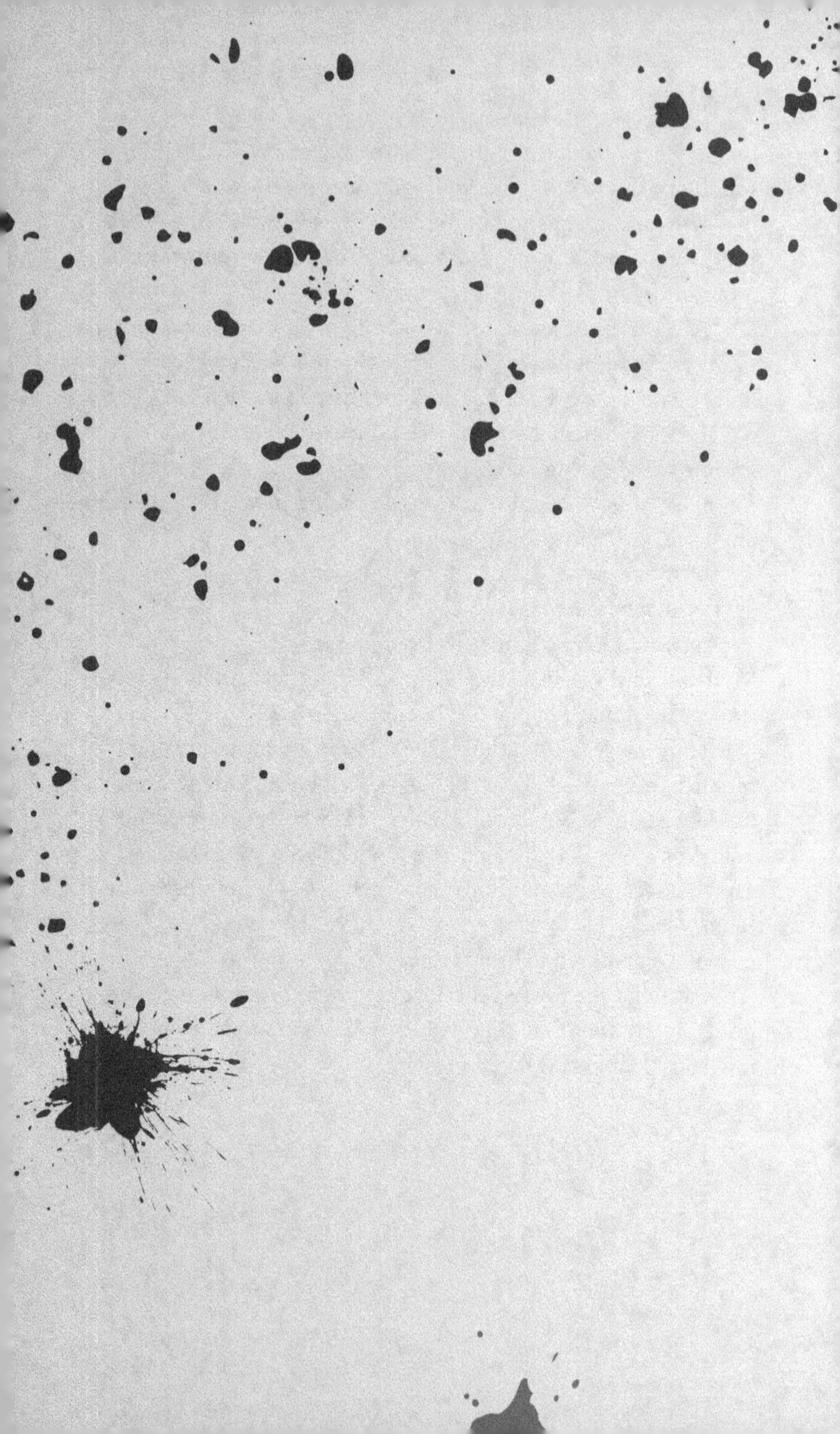

# Darfield

Terrick cried as we packed; the first time I'd ever seen tears in his normally jovial eyes.

"We'll take only what we need, lass. Nothing more," he said as he plucked a wooden doll off the shelf. He traced his fingers over the doll's face and smoothed his thumb over its braids. His lip trembled.

"Dorothy is good at drying tears," I said. I'd christened the doll with that name after Terrick and I began reading the fictional adventures of Dorothy and her dog. An exciting tale I would, sadly, never finish.

Terrick blinked and returned Dorothy to the shelf. "As much as she would doubtless enjoy the journey," he tapped his thumb against Dorothy's shoulder, "I'm afraid she isn't an essential item."

"You're sad," I murmured.

"No." He wiped his moist cheeks. "The dust is bothering my eyes." His smile was strained. "You'll never fit those clothes in your saddle bag if you fold them like that," he chuckled as he surveyed my haphazardly piled garments. "Here, lass, we'll fold them together."

His grief was palpable, even as he tried to hide it from me.

And, at the time, I hadn't understood the brevity of the situation. I didn't learn of Terrick's past until many years later.

HE'D BEEN a soldier in his youth and had helped to liberate Sakar from Ramiel's rule. While in the army, he met Lucy.

When the first war ended, and Sakar was declared free, Terrick and Lucy moved to Swindon.

As Terrick opened his fiction book shop, Lucy became a wood crafter. She designed each item of furniture in Terrick's dwelling, including the flowered armoire. After she bore Terrick a daughter, Lucy also used her skills for toy making.

The little Dorothy doll had been Lucy's creation. Their daughter had adored the doll. As had I.

Terrick had many years of happiness with his family. In that regard, he was luckier than most. But I've found happiness lowers one's pain tolerance. If one is not used to a life of anguish, they'll find themselves unable to bear the burden when tragedy strikes.

Terrick's daughter was nearing adulthood when she accompanied her mother into the forest to collect wood. It was mid-summer, and the day promised to be sunny and arid. Lucy harnessed their old horse to a cart and told Terrick she'd return before nightfall.

She did not return.

Terrick found Lucy, their daughter, and the horse the next morning. All three were drained of blood. Their murderer, a wild Púca, still stood nearby. The creature had been long abandoned by its masters and nursing a crippling injury to its left forehoof. Perhaps Lucy and her daughter had been inattentive, thinking themselves safe while close to Swindon's borders, and had been easy prey. Perhaps hunger had lent the Púca speed and drove it to ignore the pain as it hunted its meal. Regardless, the creature went to its grave with a full belly.

And Terrick lost his family.

But their shadows clung to the dark corners of his dwelling.

Haunted by the echoes of those old memories, and unable to cope with his grief, Terrick left Swindon. He spent a decade journeying across the land, collecting new books and teaching children to read. But no matter how far he traveled, or how long he stayed away, he'd always been able to call Swindon home. The memories of his family remained preserved in his dwelling, ready to welcome him when his grieving eased. And it had, for a time. I think he found some measure of happiness again when he brought me into his home.

Until I forced him to leave it again. Permanently.

And, although I didn't fully grasp what he was losing, I knew his sadness was my doing. Guilt rested upon my shoulders; heavier than any milkmaid's yolk.

This was my fault.

And I've never forgiven myself for it.

TERRICK'S FACE seemed to age another decade as he strapped our meager possessions to the saddles. He had found a livery willing to sell him two beasts: a wide-chested bay stallion and a small speckled gray pony. I think, perhaps, the livery owner was grateful we were using his animals to leave Swindon.

Terrick spared his home a parting glance before he turned to me, forcing a smile. "There, lass, didn't I tell you we'd fit all your clothes if we folded them properly? Come now, let's get you in the saddle…"

The townspeople watched as we departed on that balmy, wintry morning. Some held weapons and regarded me with mistrust and hostility as I followed Terrick through the winding streets. Words swirled through the air.

"That's not a hybrid. Mark my words."

"Seruf sent her. I'm certain of it."

"Why are we allowing it to live?"

"Well, I'll not be killin' it and riskin' Seruf's wrath."

Sobs racked through me. They spoke about me as though I were an object they'd taken an aversion to. As though I wasn't *human*.

"It's alright, lass." Terrick drew his horse alongside mine and reached over, grasping my shoulder.

I shied away from his touch. He pulled his arm back with a sigh.

Glares and whispers followed us into the forest.

"Pay no mind to what they've said," Terrick told me once we were well clear of Swindon's borders.

I sniffled and wiped my tears with the back of my hand.

"Fear is an ugly thing, lass. It often makes people say what they do not mean. You are not a monster. You are a hybrid. One…*gifted* with an unusual power."

Gifted?

I thought of Darcie and Grady's scorched bodies. "It's not a gift," I snarled.

"You may not see it as one now—"

"I *killed* Darcie." The words burned my throat.

"I know, lass. You lost control—"

"Then how can you call what I have a *gift?*" The wiry gray strands of my pony's mane blurred as moisture filled my eyes. The pony flicked his ears back, no doubt sensing my distress.

"You could do great things with your power." Terrick's voice remained steady, even as his eyes brightened with unshed tears. "You only need to learn how to control it. I can show you how, lass. We'll learn together."

Terrick's faith in me never wavered.

I only wish it had been rewarded.

DARFIELD WAS A SPRAWLING CITY.

A towering castle stood on the shoreline, overlooking a violent sea. The city streets were overcrowded: there were houses stacked on top of each other, rows upon rows of shops, and people clustered so closely together, they bumped elbows as they walked. And the sheer breadth of merchandise available was awe-inspiring.

In Swindon, we'd had one shoemaker. Darfield had thirteen. There were also fabric stores on every street in Darfield, some selling cloth in dazzling shades of reds and yellows.

I gaped at the red gown that hung in a shop window. "How did they *do* that?" I asked.

Terrick smiled. "I'm not certain. But it's quite beautiful, isn't it? And look here, lass! This one nearly matches your eyes!"

The tunic in question boasted a swirl of soft reds and blues. I pressed my nose to the glass, my eyes combing over the brilliant garment, studying every detail. The material was unlike any I'd ever seen, more resembling the calm ripples in a pool of water than the normal weaves and pulls of fabric.

Terrick squeezed my shoulder. "Ah, lass. When we have

more coin, perhaps I'll buy it for you." There was a note of worry in his voice. He'd had precious little savings when we left Swindon. But that had been several months ago, and our supply had dwindled since.

It was silly for me to covet something so needlessly expensive. But I'd never wanted anything as badly as I wanted that tunic.

Still, I reluctantly pulled myself away from it and followed Terrick through the town.

The stench of ale and the sweet aromas of smoked meat hovered in the air as we passed no less than a dozen taverns. Music seeped from pub doors. And many of those establishments were open well into the wee hours of the morning.

Darfield, I quickly learned, was a city that never slept.

But, for all its grandeur, it lacked Swindon's kindness.

In Swindon, a man with few coins could rent a room at an inn, so long as he agreed to supplement the cost with work. Darfield permitted no such exceptions. And, with our funds in dire ~~straights~~ straits, we couldn't find lodging.

We spent the first week sleeping in the stalls with our horses. In the mornings we'd wash in the water troughs, shake the straw out of our clothes, and Terrick would leave to search for employment.

"Would you like to join me?" Terrick asked each day.

And, each morning, I responded the same: "You only talk about boring things all day."

To which he would chuckle and pat the top of my head. "Well, please stay close to the stables. Darfield is a large city, lass. You can't roam as freely here as you could at Swindon."

He was incorrect in that statement.

There was *more* freedom in Darfield. The people were so consumed in their own frenzied lives, they didn't spare me a glance as I journeyed through the city. It was a relief to move about without feeling angry leers and hearing whispered accusations.

Often, I went to stare at the tunic. It had gone unsold, likely because of the exorbitant price. One hundred coins, enough to feed and house a family for a month. But the garment was utterly resplendent. There were golden ~~tassles~~ tassels on the laces. It shimmered in the sunlight. And the fabric's color changed with the position of the sun, appearing raspberry pink in the morning light, deep plum in the evenings, or on sunless days, and orchid in the afternoon.

I was ~~mesmorized~~ mesmerized. It didn't matter the tunic was made for an adult and would have been an ill fit for me. I still envisioned myself wearing it. In my imaginings, I'd stroll through the streets, the majestic material sparkling. People would notice me, undoubtedly, but for the *right* reasons. Instead of whispering about how dangerous I was, they'd murmur about how wonderful I looked…

On one warm and sunny afternoon, I became so distracted staring at the tunic, I didn't notice the boy sprinting around the corner. Not until he crashed into me.

I grunted as I fell, my shoulder colliding with the stone street. The boy landed on top of me in a heap, his gangly legs and arms entangled with mine. "Apologies," he groaned.

A few people stopped and stared but did not move to assist us. Most were too absorbed in their own worries to notice what had happened.

It took a moment for the boy to right himself—his legs were far too long for his body—and then he bent down, extending a hand toward me.

"Have you been blinded? Or are you merely daft?" I asked, refusing his offer of help and rising on my own. "Did you not see me standing here?"

"Yes," the boy's hand dropped to his side. "I did. But I

thought *you* saw *me*. I called out—" he glanced over his shoulder and, without warning, snatched my arm.

"What are you—" I began.

"Laugh." He flattened his back against the wall of the shop and spun me around until I faced him.

"What?"

"Laugh," he hissed as he crouched, ducking his head beneath mine. "Pretend I've told you a joke."

I glared at him as a throbbing pulse beat through my bruised shoulder. "I doubt I'd find any joke of yours amusing."

"Please." Sweat beaded on his brow. He was breathing heavily and his eyes—the most gorgeous blue eyes I'd ever seen—were wide.

Perhaps it was those eyes that swayed me. They were every bit as ~~mesmorizing~~ —mesmerizing as the tunic. I did as he asked, although I found it quite difficult to force a sound of glee.

"*That's* your laugh?" The boy gave me a baffled look. "You sound like a braying donkey."

I scoffed. "Perhaps if you had an ounce of charm…"

"I've more than an ounce…"

"…or wit…"

"…I also have that…"

"…you'd hear a genuine laugh. But, at the moment, I'm annoyed. So I can either continue braying or…"

The boy dropped his gaze, giving my arm a frantic squeeze. "Continue laughing. *Please.*"

As I carried on with my strained guffaw, three armored men ran past us. Soldiers. One of them grunted, "I'm sure the wee bastard went this way."

"He'll stay in the alleys," another said. "Easier for him to hide. If we turn here, we may be able to catch the blighter before he reaches the border."

My forced laugh died as the soldiers turned down another street. "Are they looking for you?" I asked the boy.

He grinned and straightened. "Looking, yes. Finding, no. Not if I can help it."

I stared at him with narrowed eyes. "Why are they hunting you?"

"I left my post."

"Why?"

"Because I don't want to be in the army." He shrugged.

"Perhaps you should have considered that before you joined."

"I didn't join. Or, rather, I didn't *choose* to." The boy cleared his throat and ran a hand through his walnut-brown hair. "Humans have the freedom to choose their profession. Hybrids don't."

"You're a hybrid?" I scoffed. This smug, lazy boy was so very much unlike Terrick, the only other hybrid I knew.

"I am. One of many. The army won't even miss me."

"If that were true, they wouldn't be searching for you."

"Well, they may miss my *ability*. Certainly not me. I am *not* a skilled fighter." He waggled his fingers in front of my face, as though offering his raw and blistered palm as evidence to his claim.

I'd gotten sores like that before too. When I first began mucking the goat pens, my hands had been ravaged by the coarse pitchfork handle. Terrick rubbed a salve on the lesions each evening, assuring me my skin would harden and I'd stop getting sores. He'd been right.

This boy clearly hadn't learned that lesson. "Perhaps if you spent more time training and less time fleeing, you would not have such blisters," I said.

"I've no wish to train. These are musician's hands, you see. I'm developing ~~callises~~ callouses in the wrong places. Soon I'll have difficulty playing the harp."

"The harp?" I asked. At the time, I couldn't picture what it was. In Swindon, some of the townspeople used flutes to carry a tune, but none possessed an instrument as grand as a harp.

"Have you never heard a harp being played?" the boy gasped.

I shook my head.

"Pity. An absolute pity. It produces such a *wondrous* sound—"

"Surely not if *you're* playing it."

"*I,*" the boy stuck out his chest proudly, "am the finest harpist in Darfield. Ask anyone. You must come with me sometime. You'll find yourself in love with—oh no," he groaned.

The soldiers had turned back onto the street and were staring at us.

"Drat." The boy straightened and gave me another beaming smile. "Luckily for me, I'm faster than them." He squeezed my arm. "You've beautiful eyes. Has anyone ever told you that?"

And, with that, he sprinted away, the soldiers pursuing him.

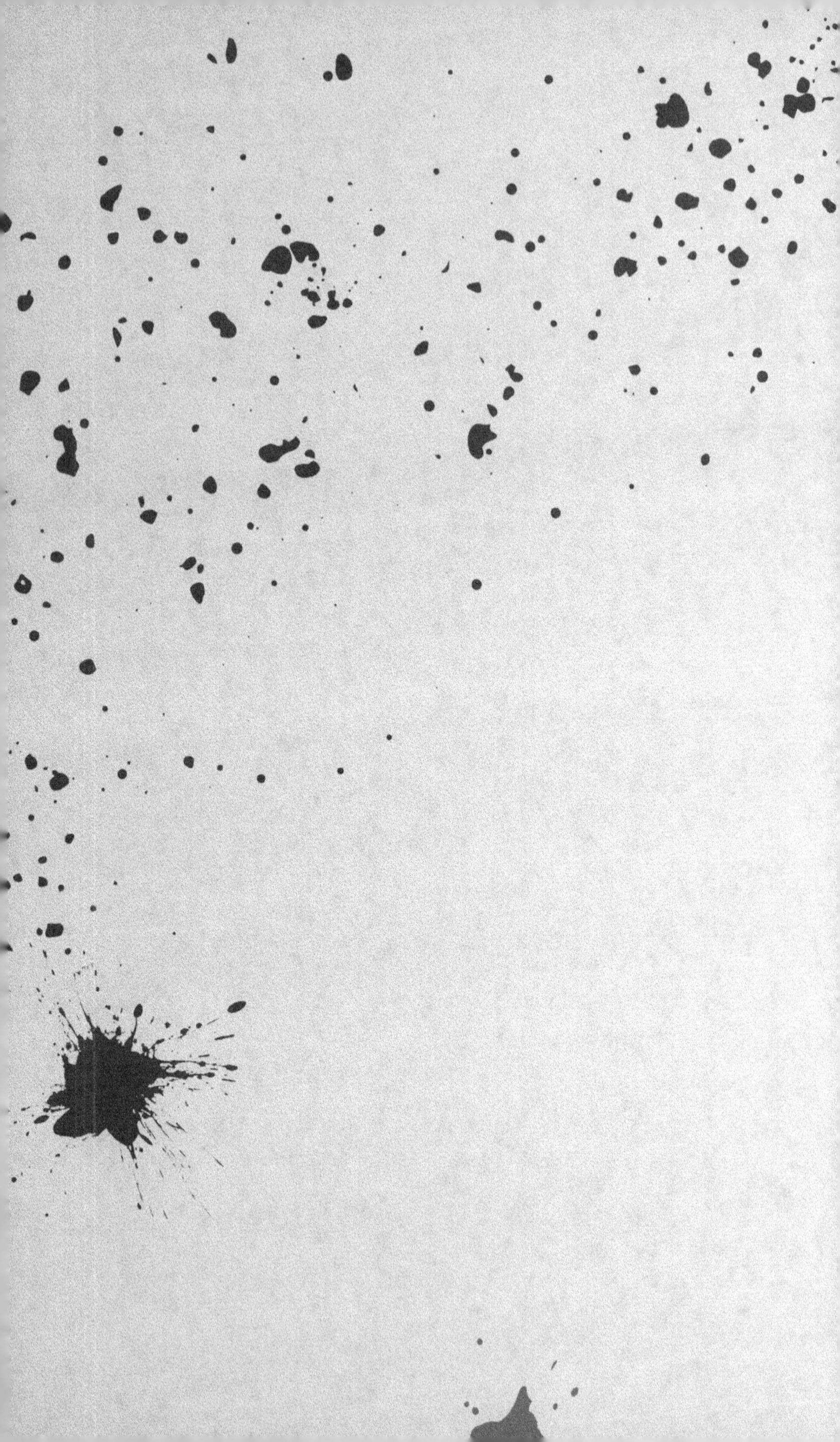

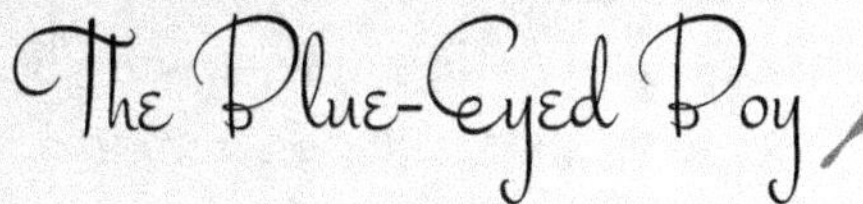

# The Blue-Eyed Boy

Terrick was suffering.

He tried to hide his sadness, but he was often slow to rise in the mornings. He laid awake late into the night, staring at the ceiling of the livery barn. Sometimes he cried, always stifling the sounds, trying not to wake me. I was, however unfortunately, a light sleeper.

Guilt ate at me. It was as though a great beast had taken residence inside my belly and was *delighting* in clawing and devouring my insides. My ability, my curse, had not only taken two lives, but it was also causing someone I loved great misery.

I wanted to bring Terrick joy. So I ventured into the crowded market, clutching onto two of the five coins we possessed, searching for something that would make him smile.

"Fish! Fresh fish! Two coins a piece!"

"Oi! What you mean it's too expensive? Think ye could make it better?"

"The price is four coins. Not three. Now get out of 'ere. I don't want to be seeing you again until ye can pay what I ask."

A swirl of voices surrounded me. Sellers shouting prices. People arguing. Haggling. This market was far larger and louder than the one in Swindon. It was overwhelming.

As was the merchandise being offered. In addition to food and clothing, one could purchase all manner of useless items. One woman, for instance, had an array of glimmering ~~jewles~~ —jewels laid out at her booth. The colorful stones were threaded with bits of string and were meant to be worn around a person's wrist, ankle, or neck. And, indeed, several women walked amongst the crowd sporting ringlets of ~~jewles~~ —jewels around their throats.

A waste of coin, to be sure. The *jewels* served no purpose and looked rather cumbersome to wear. But, as one girl exclaimed to her mother, *"they're beautiful!"*

Another merchant sold plates and cups made with decorative glass. They, at least, were functional as well as beautiful, although I wondered how practical they were. Surely glass would break easily? The standard wood and metal seemed to be the sturdier options, and there were merchants aplenty selling those as well.

As I said, the market was overwhelming.

And entirely unwelcoming.

I wandered along the streets, surveying the wares for sale at each booth, my fingers curled around my coins, which were proving to be insufficient. The prices were exorbitant.

I'd almost given up hope when I passed the cheese seller.

I paused, gaping. The remarkable cheese on display was soft and creamy, more of a liquid than a solid food.

A man and a woman stood by the booth, speaking with the vendor.

"'Tis a spread," the vendor, a gray-haired woman, said. "I make it meself, I do. Ye put it on bread, ye see?" She pulled a knife from her apron, cut a slice of bread from one of the loaves on her stand, and dipped the edge of the knife into the cheese. The creamy substance clung to the blade. "And then ye spread it." She dragged the knife over the bread, smearing cheese across the surface.

It felt as though my bottom jaw had become disconnected from the top. I couldn't stop staring. The cheese resembled a fluffy cloud as it sat atop the bread. And I wondered what it would taste like. Was it bitter, as most cheeses were? Or sweet, like milk?

The man took the first bite. "Hmm!" he exclaimed as crumbs dribbled down the front of his tunic. "Beda, this is *excellent!*"

The vendor, Beda, drew herself up proudly. "Aye, I told ye. Ye've never tasted cheese like this before, have ye? Ye— oi!"

I flinched as she whipped her head around to look at me. I'd been so ~~mesmorized~~—mesmerized by the cheese, I hadn't realized I was moving closer to her booth.

"Away with ye, child." Beda waved her arms.

"But—" I stretched my hand out, prepared to give her my coins.

"Away!" Beda squawked.

"This is hardly a way to speak to a customer—"

"If ye wish to make a purchase, come back with yer mother," Beda snapped.

"I have no mother."

"Yer father, then. Now go. Away! I have real customers to tend to." Beda marched toward me, her bony, gnarled hands flailing through the air.

Anger flared inside me. "Anyone with coin is a *real customer.*" I waved one of my coins in front of her face.

Her eyes followed the movement, but she didn't relax her stance.

"You Wicked Witch," I muttered as I closed my fist around the coin and turned away.

It was a term I'd learned from the stories Terrick had read to me in Swindon.

"What is a Wicked Witch?" I'd asked him.

"An unkind person, lass," he'd told me. "One who delights in tormenting others."

Beda's brow furrowed. She knew I'd insulted her but had likely never heard the phrase before. "Away with ye," she snapped again. "If I catch ye here again, yer knuckles'll be bleedin.'" She clutched her knife and turned to apologize to her *real customers*.

"Children," she huffed. "There's a group of 'em that are always causing me grief. Sticking their fingers in me cheese…"

My eyes and cheeks burned as I walked away. I was so angry, so disappointed, and so preoccupied with listening to her talk, that it took me a moment to notice the itch in my palms. I rubbed them against each other to alleviate the prickling, and my stomach turned to rot.

My two silver coins had melted.

I stopped, staring at my hands, which had grown hot enough to liquefy silver. There were no flames yet. But the itching beneath my skin grew.

Panic swelled inside me. I couldn't stay here! People brushed against my arms as they navigated the congested market. I would hurt someone!

My breath escaped in ragged gasps as I staggered off the street, going behind a line of booths and stumbling into the stone wall of a nearby building. I clutched a hand to my chest, willing the itch to subside…

And then I heard the sound.

It was a sharp noise, bordering on shrill. Melodic. Haunting. Music, clearly, but unlike any I had ever heard before. It caused a strange stirring in my chest; a tingling sensation one normally feels before they're about to laugh. Or, perhaps, cry.

The itch eased. The tight, dreadful sensation in my stomach quieted, as though the emotive melody had swept it away.

I turned, desperate to find the source of the music.

And I saw him through the half-open door of a tavern. He sat beside a large wooden sculpture, his fingers dancing over the strings stretched through the center of the instrument. His head was bowed, and his hair obscured much of his face, but I knew it was him. The blue-eyed boy.

He was every bit as talented as he'd claimed to be.

The sounds he produced from that wooden sculpture— the *harp*, as he'd called it—were hypnotizing. Both hopeful and heartbreaking. Upbeat and sorrowful. I never knew a simple tune could induce two polarizing emotions at once.

I was not the only one entranced. Indeed, there were several people inside the tavern watching him intently, their drinks and meals forgotten. A few others had paused their market perusal to listen as well.

The boy didn't seem to notice he'd garnered an audience. Or, perhaps, he didn't care. He kept his head down, his eyes closed, as his fingers plucked at the delicate strings. Each chord produced a distinct note, some shriller than others. Under an inexperienced hand, the instrument may have sounded grating. But, beneath the boy's nimble fingers, it was…

~~Magikal~~—Magical.

Another word from Terrick's fiction books: something extraordinary. Otherworldly.

*Magical.*

I didn't know how long I stood there. A few minutes, at least. The market life swirled around me, but I paid it no heed. I was unable to tear my eyes away from the blue-eyed boy who produced such wondrous music.

"There he is. The impudent child..." A harsh voice drifted over my head.

Two men, both clad in leather armor and wearing swords at their belts, walked past me.

Soldiers.

My belly clenched.

They were heading toward the tavern. And the blue-eyed boy.

*I've no wish to train.* The boy once said. Now I understood why. For his hands, capable of creating such captivating, ~~melodius~~—melodious sounds, were surely ill-equipped to hold a weapon.

I did not pause to consider my actions. I merely threw myself forward, colliding with the backside of one of the soldiers, and loosed an agonized wail.

The soldiers turned.

A few people stopped and stared. Most importantly, the boy ceased playing. He watched me through the open tavern door, his eyes wide.

"Are you alright?" The young soldier who knelt beside me had a patchy beard and a kind face.

My eyes watered. 'Twas not me summoning fake tears—I do not have such a talent. I'd wrenched my right knee and was genuinely in pain.

The soldier reached for me, likely to place a hand on my shoulder.

But I thought of the melted coins in my palm and drew back, further twisting my aching knee.

"Child?" The soldier prompted.

Through my blurred vision, I saw the blue-eyed boy scramble away from the harp, sprinting to the back of the tavern.

I only needed to keep the soldiers' attention on me a moment longer.

"She was," I sniffled, "cruel to me."

The soldier's brow furrowed. "Who?"

"T-the woman w-with the c-cheese."

"That'd be Beda." The other soldier sighed. Age lines creased his brow, and his dark brown hair had begun to gray. "Stealin', were ya?" he asked me.

"No," I said.

He scoffed. "And what other cause would she have to— Oi! The wee bastard's gone. *Again.* Leave the child be, Connor. If she was stealin', old Beda will have taught her a lesson."

With a somewhat reluctant sigh, the young soldier, Connor, stood and followed his companion into the tavern.

I'd given the blue-eyed boy a chance to escape. Mere seconds, but I hoped it was enough.

My knee throbbed. I returned to my feet with a wince and limped to the other side of the street. A few people stared but did not offer to help. Nearby vendors guarded their wares and peered at me with heedful eyes.

Each step was agony. I made it only a short distance before I stopped, leaning against a wall that divided a bakery and fabrics shop. The ache did not subside, and my knee had developed a rapidly beating pulse.

"Have you hurt yourself?"

I flinched when a voice sounded beside my left ear.

The blue-eyed boy leaned against the wall next to me, a smug smile stretched across his lips.

A strange, quivering emotion gripped my insides. "Are you daft?" I asked. "Those soldiers were just here!"

"And now they're two blocks away, likely thinking they'll catch me at the next tavern. Although they *would* have caught me at this one, had you not started squealing like a pig."

"I did not *squeal!*"

The boy's grin widened. "You've quite the flair for dramatics, eh? But I saw the way you landed. It's the right knee you injured, yes?" He stretched a hand toward me.

I sidled sideways, evading his touch.

His smile faded. "I'll not harm you," he said.

*But* I *may harm* you. The thought passed through my mind, though I dared not say it out loud.

He reached for me again.

I moved again.

He frowned. "Do you fear me?"

"Of course not."

"Then why do you cower?"

"I don't." I raised my chin defiantly. This time, when he reached for me, I forced myself to be still. I didn't breathe, terrified any miniscule movement would send the fire spiraling out of control.

The boy brushed his fingers against my forehead. His hands, despite the clusters of blisters, were tender. Kind.

The touch lasted only a second.

I exhaled, trying not to seem pleased when he put a distance between us again. And it was only after relief seeped into my muscles that I realized my knee was no longer aching.

"You're a Healer!" I gasped. Terrick had told me of the Healers—the most coveted hybrids in all of Sakar.

The boy waggled his fingers. "I am...*unfortunately.*" He huffed and swiped a lock of hair out of his eyes. "Now, tell me, did the sobbing only begin *after* you injured your knee? Or were you weeping for joy upon hearing my music?"

"Weeping for joy?" I scoffed. Of course, his melodies had brought me close to tears, but I thought it best not to inflate his ego further.

"Don't worry, you aren't the only girl in Darfield to find herself overwhelmed while watching me play." He grinned.

The boy *reeked* of arrogance. But there was gentleness in him too.

He was aggravating.

And yet, I laughed. Something I hadn't done for many months. Not since the *incident*. "Perhaps I was *weeping*," I giggled, "because your ham-handed playing made my ears bleed. Have you considered that?"

The boy chuckled and leaned toward me, a devious glint in his eye. "I don't believe you would've been so quick to intervene on my behalf if you found my playing 'ham-handed.'" His eyes twinkled. "Your pig-squealing was intentional, was it not? To warn me?"

Again, I raised my chin, reluctant to admit the truth. "I had to do something to drown out your wretched playing."

He threw his head back with a guffaw. "Either way, you've given me time I wouldn't have otherwise had to myself. And I think I'll use it to help you." He winked. "I heard you had a run-in with Beda. Mad old woman. Convinced children are creatures sent by Ramiel to destroy her merchandise. I," he thumped his hand against his scrawny chest, "can get the creamy cheese you seek. But I'll not be doing it for free, mind."

"And why not? I helped you without expecting repayment."

"Ah, so you're admitting to helping me!" His eyes glimmered.

"Well," I cleared my suddenly parched throat, "did you not say my pig-squealing gave you time to escape?"

"It did. But then you insulted me, so the good deed has soured a bit. Hence why I'm still willing to help you, but at a cost. If I succeed," he pursed his lips, "you shall come watch me play again, *without* the sarcastic banter. Tomorrow night, at Elton's tavern."

"And if you fail?" I raised my eyebrow.

"Then you, dear lady, shall still come watch me play, but you may make all the delightful sarcastic quips you'd like." He held out his hand. "Have we a deal?"

I laughed again and almost placed my palm in his without a second thought. But a glint of silver, caught between my index and middle finger, drew my eye. The last remnants of my precious coins, melted into a crevice.

I hesitated, drawing my hand back. "I don't have any coin to offer her. Or you." I curled my fingers into a fist, hoping he wouldn't see the flecks of silver.

The boy watched me, the expression in his eyes softening.

"It's...Ter...my father," I said. "He's been searching for employment..."

"There's no need to explain," the boy's voice gentled. And then his lips curled upward once again. "It'll only sweeten the deal. If I should succeed in securing your creamy cheese, *free of charge*, you shall come with me tomorrow night and," he dropped his voice to a whisper, "you'll tell me about this power you're trying to conceal."

I drew back as though he'd slapped me. "How dare—"

"Your secret would be safe with me," he added hastily. "I'll not speak of it to anyone. Certainly not the *army*." He shuddered. "You're too spirited. The army is so...dull. It would be a crime to see them extinguish your *spark*."

My heart fluttered. A bead of sweat dripped down my back. He knew. He *had* to. Why else would he have chosen those last few words?

But the boy only maintained a patient smile, waiting for me to respond.

If he didn't know about my curse, would he treat me more harshly once he discovered what I could do?

Or would he still wish to be my friend?

I swallowed and placed my other hand in his.

He would learn the truth eventually. Perhaps it would be best if I told him first.

"You have yourself a deal," I said. My mouth felt odd—too dry. And my tongue seemed to have grown to twice its size.

The boy barked out a laugh and, to my very great surprise, kissed my knuckles.

It was an odd sensation, having a boy's lips pressed against my skin. Odd, but not unpleasant. His mouth was warm and soft. His breath tickled.

A storm of conflicting emotions filled my chest. But, before I could berate the boy for his forwardness, or properly analyze why his kiss made my innards quiver, he whirled away, heading to Beda's stand.

I did not follow. One encounter with the old woman had been quite enough. So I waited, watching the endless wave of people moving through the streets. The moments passed tediously. After a while, I moved away from the wall, thinking the boy had failed and didn't want to bruise his pride by admitting defeat.

At that moment, he emerged from the opposite direction. He was panting, his face red and gleaming with sweat.

"Did you lose your way?" I asked.

He shook his head. "Soldiers." He glanced over his shoulder. "Drat. I can't stay." He pressed a square package, wrapped in leaves, into my hand. "Tomorrow night," he rasped. "Meet me here. I'll walk with you to the tavern." His eyes were alight with excitement, even as he sprinted away.

THE CHEESE WAS UTTERLY *DELIGHTFUL*. Sweeter than milk.

"Lass," Terrick groaned in bliss. "Where did you *get* this?" He licked the creamy cheese off his fingers—we hadn't any bread to spread the cheese onto, so we'd simply dipped our fingers into the box.

"A friend," I said. I couldn't keep the smile off my face as I thought of the blue-eyed boy.

"A friend?" Terrick repeated, his face glowing with joy. "You've made a friend already? That's *wonderful*, lass! Hmm…" he took another bite. "Please tell your friend they're welcome to gift us with this cheese anytime they're feeling charitable."

"He didn't gift it," I mumbled. "He merely helped me to buy the cheese. I took two of our coins." My face heated. "I'm sorry."

Terrick's smile did not wane. "Well, your friend certainly helped you spend those coins wisely. This is a *delicacy*. And there's enough here to last a few days." He patted my knee. "Thank you, lass. This was a treat."

I went to sleep that night with a full belly. As I curled into my bed of straw, listening to my pony shuffle about, I imagined what a friendship with the blue-eyed boy might look like; what adventures we could experience together.

But, as my waking thought melted into a dream, the images changed. I saw the blue-eyed boy screaming in terror and agony as his skin blistered. I saw myself standing before him, flames dancing over my fingers. The people of Darfield clustered around me, crying out in fear—

"Lass!"

Flames greeted me when I opened my eyes. They were consuming the stable.

The horses screeched in panic as embers fell from the burning ceiling. Smoke swirled; Terrick choked on it as he leaned over me. "Lass!" He touched my arm and cried out when his hand burnt.

Fire rippled across my skin. My clothes had disintegrated, as had my straw bed. And the fire continued to spread, and spread, and spread....

"I'm sorry, lass," Terrick coughed and sputtered. He raised a knife over his head, his eyes watering. "I'm sorry." He drove the handle into my temple, rendering me ~~unconcious~~ unconscious.

I WASN'T BLAMED for the fire.

A stableboy had left a candle in the hayloft. According to the rumors, at least. I'm certain Terrick was the source of that falsity. But no one questioned it. Flames and straw were a deadly mixture, after all. And, with people from the neighboring houses and shops working together to extinguish the flames and rescue those trapped inside, no human or equine lives were lost.

It should have been a relief.

But it wasn't.

I'd nearly killed again. And that night began the longest and most miserable stretch of my life.

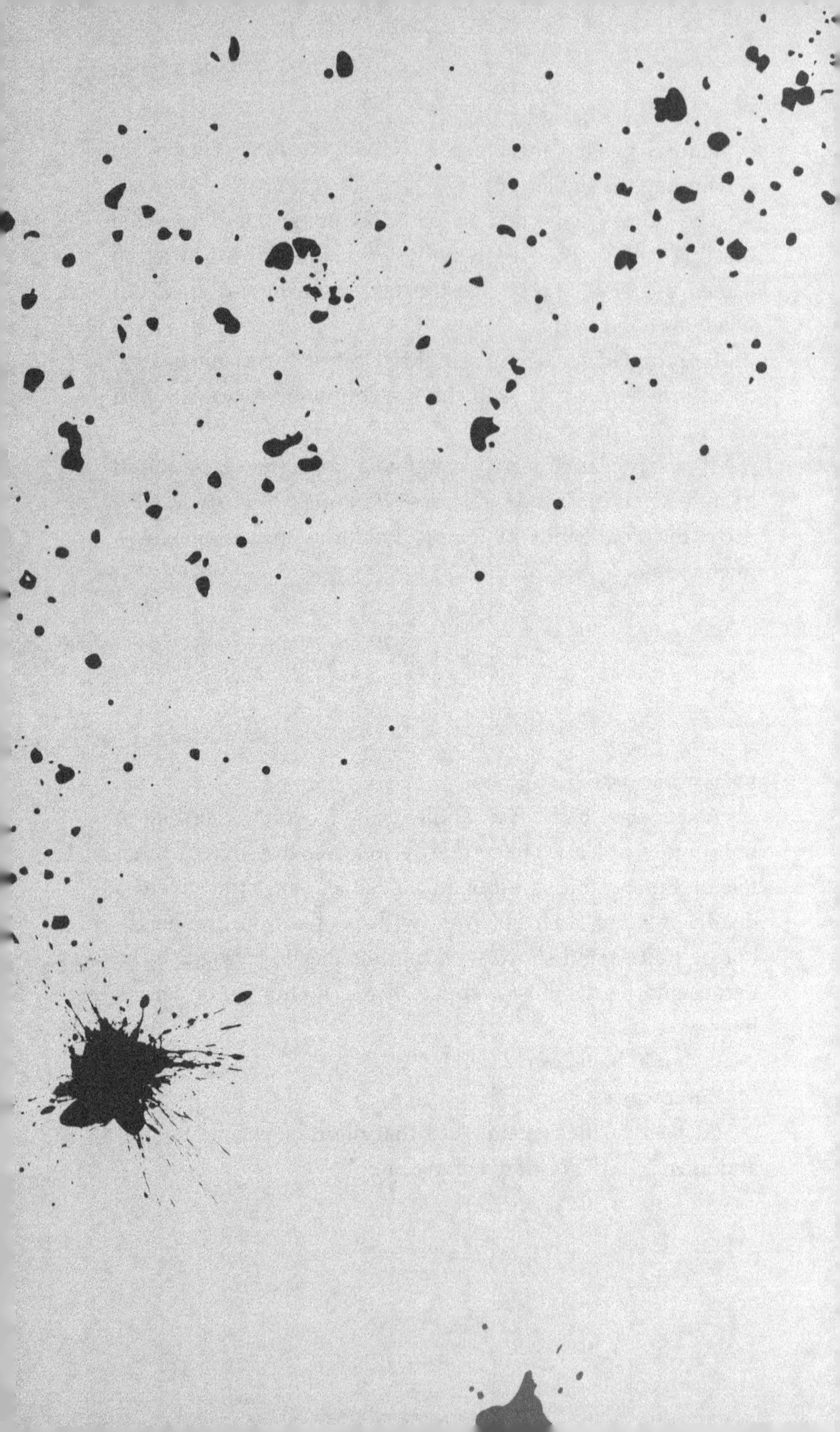

# Lost Years

I should pause my tale here to make something clear.

This part of my life was rather *unkind*. Almost cruel. But I do not, nor will I *ever*, blame Terrick.

He could not teach me to control a volatile ability he didn't understand. If he'd sought help, Darfield's soldiers would have taken me away. I likely would have been forced to join the army. But Terrick feared a worse fate and did not want to see me tortured.

Moving to another city would have only provided a temporary reprieve. As long as the cursed fire ran through my veins, Terrick and I would not have been accepted anywhere.

So Terrick did what he could to ensure I had a home, and I was safe, even if it came with a cost.

Terrick was a kind man with a big heart. Cruelty had never been his intention. He simply didn't know what else to do.

MY DESCENT into misery started simply enough.

"This tonic will help you sleep," Terrick told me.

We were staying in yet another livery stable, our horses tied a few feet away from us. My little speckled pony had a burn mark on his left flank. I hadn't been able to stop staring at it.

It had been a full day since my fire ravaged the stables.

"I don't want to sleep," I mumbled.

"You must, lass," Terrick coaxed. "The tonic will keep the dreams away. You won't hurt anyone else. I promise."

And it *did* keep the dreams away. For a while.

Months passed.

Terrick found employment at a tannery. I hated him working there. It demanded too much from his age-ravaged body. But we needed the coin.

His new position also came with lodging: a small room on the top of the shop.

When we moved into our new dwelling, Terrick wrapped me in a threadbare blanket and kept his arm around my shoulders as we climbed the stairs. "My child," he'd said to our new landlord. "She's quite ill."

In hindsight, I should have questioned his motives. I was perfectly healthy. If our landlord had spared me more than a passing glance, he would have seen that. But, at the time, I'd closed my eyes, wishing I could disappear.

And I did. Terrick was, after all, a gifted Concealer. Even when he did not use his power.

I SPENT four years in Darfield, trapped in that small, ~~claustrofobic~~ claustrophobic room above the tannery, barred from the outside world.

That hadn't been Terrick's intention. He'd meant my situation to be temporary while he searched for a solution to my ever-growing power.

"Perhaps it is linked to your emotions," he said one afternoon. "Your power seems to be at its strongest in the presence of fear or anger. If I can teach you to school your emotions…I once had several books that discussed this very topic." A hint of sadness crept into his voice.

I turned away, burying my face in my sleeve to hide my tears.

Terrick was correct, but it is not an easy thing to control one's emotions. The more one tries to restrain them, the harder they fight. The more one restricts them, the faster they gallop out of control.

As the tonic lost its ~~eficacy~~ efficacy, the dreams returned. My brain delighted in tormenting me with horrific images while I slept, and it gave my hated power ample opportunity to seize control.

Terrick became adept at recognizing the signs, and always woke me before my fire damaged the building. But, in doing so, he wounded himself. Burns marred his palms and arms.

Every time I stared at his mottled skin, my stomach turned to rot. My panic grew. It's an awful thing when you fear yourself. There's no way to escape. No relief from the constant churning of anxiety in your gut, or the horrifying images that run unbridled through your mind.

I'd never been so terrified. Even on that day in Detha, as I'd waited to be cooked, I did not experience the same intensity of terror that I felt during my time in Darfield.

Terrick tried to help. He gave me meditation exercises to "purge my mind of negative thoughts." He also taught me a stretching exercise he called *yoga,* which was meant to calm my mind.

They didn't work.

As my fear grew, and my power became more temperamental, Terrick turned to the tonic, increasing its potency.

When I drank the tonic, my mind became blessedly blank. My emotions numbed. Sleep came easily, and I slumbered deeply, never dreaming. But wakefulness became more and more difficult. Even when I was awake, I was rarely alert. A permanent cloud seemed to hover over my eyes. My brain sometimes struggled to form coherent thoughts. The days, weeks, months, and years passed in a blur.

Once, I remembered being startled by the snow falling outside because my last clear-headed memory had been of summer. The seasons had changed, twice, without me noticing.

I never left the room.

Terrick maintained the lie that I was his ailing daughter and was too sick to leave bed. No one questioned him.

He spent his days laboring at the tannery. At night he returned, damp and dingy and smelling of alkaline and ash. If I was awake, he'd eat his supper with me, often telling me the stories he'd learned from his fiction books. I'm sad to say I don't remember any of them.

On my clear-headed days, I noted how quickly he was aging; his skin sagged more and more, and his hair turned whiter and whiter. Sometimes, he stared at me with tears in his eyes and desperation etched into his face. He hated what he was doing to me. He would try to make up for it, using his spare coins to buy me things: wooden dolls, cheeses in a variety of flavors, hair pins, or ~~jewles~~ jewels. At one point, he procured the beautiful tunic I'd once spent so many hours admiring. Surely, he had saved his coin for months to afford such an exorbitant gift.

And I couldn't summon the energy to wear it. Truthfully, I don't recall when I received it. I simply noticed it one day, hanging in the armoire, its dazzling color muted in our poorly lit room.

The last years of my childhood slipped away. I spent my days sitting by the window, dully watching the world change.

Often, I saw the blue-eyed boy, always dressed in military leathers, as he visited the shops on our street. It seemed he'd given up his quest to leave the army. He'd grown into his too-long limbs, although his frame remained thin and somewhat gangly. His smug smile faded, replaced by a grim expression that aged him beyond his years. It made me sad.

I wanted to hear his music again.

If I went down to him, would he play the harp for me? Would his smile return? Would he accept my apology for not upholding my end of the wager?

I wanted to speak with him. Desperately. But I never did.

As I began the path toward adulthood, my power grew with me. The tonic lost its ~~effacy~~ efficacy again and my dreams returned with renewed vigor.

Every night I woke screaming, fire erupting from my fingertips.

Every night, Terrick rendered me ~~unconcious~~ unconscious, usually by wrapping his arm around my shoulders and applying pressure to the sides of my neck. It caused a momentary flash of panic as my airways were restricted, but then I slid into darkness. And the fire retreated.

It was a barbaric system. But it worked.

For a time.

Terrick was old. And those four years were as unkind to him as they were to me. Between the guilt that weighed on him and the strain of his tannery duties, his days on earth were rapidly ending.

It happened on an autumn eve.

I'd been having a clear-headed day. Enough to notice the blue-eyed boy, fully into adulthood now, walking with a woman on his arm. He smiled again. Maybe not as vibrantly as he had a few years prior, but he smiled. A hot, dark feeling coiled in my chest. Jealousy. I hated that girl, with her shimmering black hair; *hated* that she'd been the one to bring the light back into his eyes. In another world, it would have been *me* clutching onto his arm as he strolled through the streets. It would have been my voice making him smile and laugh.

I cried when the boy left my sight. Although I made sure my tears were dry when Terrick returned that evening.

Terrick moved slowly, pausing on every third step up to our room. When he walked through the door, he was winded. His face was pale, and a blue vein pulsed at his temple.

"Ah, lass," he gasped as he heaved himself into the nearest chair. "Give me a moment to catch my breath, and then we shall eat. I've thought of a good story to share with you; one of my favorites from childhood."

He never caught his breath.

Even as I spooned broth into his bowl, he wheezed. His hands shook.

"Perhaps the day fatigued me more than I thought," he said when I asked if he was ill. Speaking brought on a violent coughing fit that left him red-faced and teary-eyed.

I placed a hand on his shoulder. There was a chill on his skin, and it wouldn't go away, no matter how many times I tried to create friction to warm him.

"I'm sorry, lass," he whispered. "The story will have to wait for another night."

I helped him to his bed. Afterward, when the cloud seeped across my vision again, and the energy left my body, I curled onto my mattress, asleep before my head hit the pillow.

I didn't take the tonic.

And the dreams returned.

I was back in Swindon, listening to Darcie scream. The acrid smell of burnt flesh rose to my nostrils, churning my stomach. Flames danced across my fingertips, growing, and growing, and growing until Darcie was consumed in the blaze.

*"Stop! Please!"* She cried.

I stared at my trembling fingers. No matter what I did, no matter how hard I tried to will it away, the fire kept growing. "I-I can't!"

*"Please..."*

"Go away," I moaned at the inferno. "Please, go *away*. I don't want this!"

*"Please, love."*

I gasped. It was no longer Darcie speaking.

It was Mama, now trapped in the swirling fire.

"Mama!" I screamed. "Mama, something's wrong—a Celestial did something to me. But I *don't want this*! Tell me how to stop it!"

She stared at me, her flesh blackening, and bubbling tears seeping from her eyes. *"It's your fault I'm dead, love,"* she rasped.

The flames grew. "I didn't—"

*"You didn't kill me, but you might as well have. I could have left Detha and gone to Sakar. If only I hadn't been cursed with another mouth to feed."*

A sickening pain speared my chest. "Mama—"

She coughed. Blood dribbled down her chin. *"I should have Offered you to the Wraiths when you were born."*

I awoke with a blood-curdling screech, which morphed into a cry of panic.

Flames engulfed the room. They roared across the ceiling and along the walls, disintegrating everything in their path. The smoke was thick; I could hardly see past the tip of my nose.

"Terrick!" I screamed.

Dimly, I heard shouts coming from outside.

"The tannery!"

"Water! Fetch water!"

"Terrick!" I dropped to the floor in a crumbled heap and crawled. "*Terrick!*"

And then I found him, lying face down on the ground, a mere three steps away from my bed. "*Terrick!*" It took all my strength to turn him over.

His eyes were open but glassy and unfocused. "Terrick!" I shook him, tugged on his arms, screamed into his ears—I did whatever I could think of to rouse him. He remained still and lifeless.

He'd died trying to wake me from my nightmare.

And, while I understand now that his demise was not my doing—his heart was failing long before that torturous night —at the time, only one thought possessed my mind: *I killed him.*

I wanted to die too. For what was the point of living? The fire had taken *everything* from me. As long as it held me in its wicked clutches, it would continue to steal everything I loved and cared for.

I sobbed as I curled beside Terrick's body. I pressed my face into his chest as the flames roared around us, consuming the building. And I pleaded for the fire to take me.

The fire, of course, would not harm me. It couldn't.

# Monster

I remembered falling.

As the floor of our room collapsed, Terrick and I tumbled down, and down, and down. The impact rattled every bone in my body and left me screaming in agony, but I never loosened my grip on Terrick. The building crumbled around us. Wood splintered. Leather burned. The tannery owner and his family were trapped inside. The stench of their singed flesh hovered like a cloud in the air.

In my arms, Terrick melted. His eyes frothed and disintegrated. His skin blistered, blackened, and turned to ash. I held onto him, even when all I had left were charred pieces of bone.

In the end, the city people found me, unclothed but unharmed, hovering over the skeleton of the only father figure I had ever known.

Voices rang out.

"Is that Terrick's child?"

"Can't be. Didn't he say she was too weak to leave bed?"

"Been dying for years as I 'eard it."

I crouched lower, wishing they would go away.

They encircled me, stepping over the wreckage. They weren't fearful, but they didn't have a reason to be. Terrick had kept me and my curse well-concealed during our time in Darfield.

"Are you alright?" A hand touched my bare shoulder.

I backed away with a scream. The fire had dwindled to a mere flicker at my fingertips, but the itch beneath my skin remained.

"How did you escape?" A man asked.

Nausea coiled in my belly. A sob suffocated me, even as my eyes remained dry. But my numb fingers maintained their iron-clad grip on Terrick's corpse.

"Come away, child." More hands touched my shoulders, guiding me away from Terrick.

"No," I rasped.

"There's nothing to fear. You're safe now."

Safe? I'd never be *safe* again. Not when the thing I feared most was myself.

"Your father's gone, child. I'm sorry."

They wouldn't *stop*.

The itch beneath my skin grew.

Hands touched mine, prying my fingers from Terrick's skeleton. Someone else patted my shoulder. Yet another person combed their fingers through my hair.

"Don't *touch me!*" The scream exploded from my throat, accompanied by a rush of fire spreading along my arms and torso.

Those attempting to comfort me were the first to die. Their pained cries rang into the night air as they burned.

*Run.*

I stared at the ~~massacer~~—massacre before me, my chest painfully tight.

Not all perished. Some had wisely stood out of the flame's reach. They ran, likely to spread the news of the tannery's destruction. And I heard the word they all whispered.

*Monster.*

Another term I'd learned from Terrick's fiction books. This one had two meanings: a strange and horrible creature, or a human capable of great wickedness.

I was both.

*Monster.*

My stomach heaved. I must have vomited—the sticky taste of bile coated my tongue—but I didn't remember. A fog crept across my brain, distorting my thoughts. My body moved stiffly and on its own accord, as though another entity had taken control of my limbs.

As I stood to flee, I noticed something shiny rippling in the cold autumn wind.

The tunic.

It lay draped over the crumbled wooden beams of the building. It was whole. Unburnt. Its colors dazzled even through the smoky haze. I staggered to it. Shards of wood, stone, and glass cut into my bare feet, but I felt no pain.

How had the tunic survived?

It had been hanging in the armoire when the fire started and should have burned with the rest of our belongings.

My flame-wrapped fingers stretched out. The fabric was cool to the touch, unbothered by my fire.

I peeled the tunic away from the wooden beam and slipped it over my head. It was, as I'd once suspected, made for an adult, and for someone with a much larger frame than mine. The sleeves cascaded beyond my fingertips, the hem brushed against my shins, and I had to re-wrap the laces—an arduous task with my hands so unsteady—to close the front over my chest.

The tunic did not disintegrate, even as the fire continued to twirl over my skin.

I staggered through the city streets, my bloodied feet slipping on the stone. People screamed when I passed them. I wrapped my arms around my chest, shivering. When the fire left me several minutes later, I missed it. A wretched curse it may have been, but it had provided some measure of protection against the cold.

I wandered, hardly aware of which direction I traveled in. And I heard more shouting; cries that a Celestial had attacked Darfield.

"The tannery…did you see what it did to the tannery?"

"It looks like a *child!*"

"Can Celestials change their form?"

My vision blurred. I sulked in the shadows, slipping into narrow alleys whenever I saw people approaching. They were hunting me now. I had to leave.

And yet, the thought of fleeing made my chest hurt.

My time at Darfield had certainly not been kind. The years had produced few good memories. But I'd had a home in this city. I'd had someone who loved me and had tried to do what was best for me. That was gone now. I was barely into adulthood (only seventeen if my estimates are correct) and I was alone.

My options were bleak. The humans' hatred for Wraiths and Celestials ran deep. If I stayed, I'd undoubtedly be tortured to a slow, ~~excrutiating~~ excruciating death. Which should have frightened me, but it didn't. I didn't care what they did to me.

I worried what *I* would do to *them*.

Seven soldiers rushed by my alleyway. They didn't notice me; their eyes focused on the plume of smoke rising from where the tannery had once been. I waited, holding my breath. When the sound of their footsteps faded, I emerged from the shadows—

And gasped as rough hands encircled my arms.

The fingers tightened, spinning me around, bringing me face-to-face with my captor.

The blue-eyed boy.

But a boy no longer.

I knew he'd grown but witnessing the changes from my bedroom window wasn't as shocking as observing them up close. He was taller than I remembered; the tip of my head only reached his chest. Bands of muscle corded around his arms. A thick coat of dark whiskers obscured much of his face. But his brilliant eyes were the same, even as they regarded me with apprehension.

"So it's you," he said, still grasping my arms. "The girl with the flair for dramatics."

I gaped at him, unable to speak.

"I waited for you," he murmured. "But I never saw you again. I did not believe you the type to dishonor a fairly won wager, so I thought something had happened and perhaps you'd left the city."

My breathing turned ragged.

"Yet you've been here all this time?" There was no malice in his eyes. Only confusion.

*I was locked away,* I wanted to say. *Locked away so I couldn't hurt anyone.* But the words wouldn't form.

The boy's brow furrowed. "What happened to you? Where are the sarcastic quips that once rested on your tongue?"

"Where is the careless smile that once brightened your face?"

I didn't realize I'd spoken out loud until the boy sighed, his hold on my arms softening. "Long gone," he said. "The army extinguishes a person's spirit. And I am, first and foremost, a soldier in Darfield's army." His voice sounded flat. Dull. "We've—*I've* been ordered to detain you. Dúnlang will question you. He's a Shield, you understand. Your power may not work on him. In fact, he's counting on its ~~ineffacy~~ inefficacy against his ability." His frown deepened. "You've killed innocent people tonight."

It hurt to meet his gaze; especially since he understood the full gravity of what I'd done.

"They say you're evil," the boy said.

*I am.* Tears burned my eyes.

"I don't believe that."

My head snapped up.

He laid his hand on my shoulder, his touch gentle. "An evil creature," he whispered, "would not show such remorse." He used his thumb to wipe a tear from my cheek. It was a tender gesture, and it only made me cry harder.

His touch terrified me. I wanted him to leave. To run. Before my fire consumed him too.

I also yearned to lean into his hand; to feel the scrape of his work-roughened fingers against my skin.

"You are Terrick's daughter?" the boy asked. "His *supposedly* ill child?"

I nodded.

"How long have you had your ability?"

I stared at my bare feet, saying nothing.

"Those were melted coins in your hand that day in the market, were they not? No," he smiled at my bemused look, "I have not forgotten. At the time, I thought you were an Illuminator; they've been known to generate enough heat to melt a coin. I didn't know…" he inhaled. "You can't control your power, can you?"

I stayed silent.

"Were you *ever* able to control it?"

Again, I did not speak.

The boy sighed again. "I'm sorry," he said. "Drat it all. Did —the things I said—did I frighten you away when I spoke of the army? Is that why you and Terrick never sought help?

Dúnlang is a pompous blaggard, and I would not wish you to meet him. But Ellard, the Celestial—*no*, he's not like The Conqueror," the boy added when I made a strangled sound. "Ellard helps protect Sakar. He's fair. And kind. He would've helped you. *I* would have helped you."

A tremor coursed through me. I didn't know what hurt more. That the boy still remembered me, even after four years. Or that help had been so close. I'd only had to go down to him, as I'd yearned to do countless times while I was confined above the tannery.

Shouts reverberated off the buildings.

I flinched. The boy drew in a long breath. "It's too late now," he said. "Ellard has been away for several months, and Dúnlang will not allow you to live." Sadness crept into his eyes as he dropped his hand and wrapped his fingers around my knuckles. "Come with me."

I wrenched my hand away.

The boy's eyes softened. The laugh that escaped him was thin. Nervous. "Allow me to clarify…come with me so I can show you a safe way out of the city. I've no wish to take you to Dúnlang."

"No? He's your commanding officer."

"Indeed."

"Yet you would defy his orders to help me escape?"

"Yes."

I glowered at him. "Why?"

The boy lowered his head and winked. "Defying an order is more entertaining than obeying it. And I still like your spark." His mouth curled into a smile. "I don't want to see Dúnlang extinguish it."

Trusting him was foolish. He might have led me right to his commander. Or, worse yet, I might've loosed my power on him. But the flame no longer pressed against my skin. And I did not care if the boy brought me to my doom. I only wished this nightmarish evening to end. So I threaded my fingers through his—his hand was wondrously warm—and allowed him to lead me away.

He followed the same pattern as I had: lingering in the shadows, hiding whenever footsteps approached. After several tense moments, we reached the edge of the city, where a narrow river trickled behind the rows of houses.

The blue-eyed boy stepped up to the water's edge.

I stopped, my heels digging into the damp grass and soft soil. I remembered all too well the terror of drowning, the pain as I inhaled water, filling my lungs until they seemed ready to burst.

"It's alright," the boy said.

"I-I can't…"

"Swim?"

I nodded.

"You don't have to." He let go of my hand and stepped into the stream. The water lapped at his ankles. "It's shallow here and won't deepen until you've reached the river. You'll know when you've arrived; the water swirls in reverse. That is your destination." He glanced at me, as though to make sure I was listening. "Follow this to the river and then walk along the bank. It's a seven-day journey, by foot, to Vaporia. You will find food and supplies there, but I don't recommend you linger. Dúnlang will send soldiers to search for you. Continue following the river until it tapers off in Wyncook Forest. From there, it's but a few days' journey to Niall. You'll be safe there. And Niall is easily recognizable—the Celestials built the fortress. It is a *resplendent* sight to behold." His eyes shone with excitement as he reminisced. "Ah, sometimes I wish I could be as eloquent with my words as I once was with my music."

*As I once was.* "Do you still play?" I asked.

The boy, who'd begun walking out of the water, glanced at me. "Pardon?"

"The harp. The last we'd met, you wanted to leave the army—"

"Because I was a musician, not a soldier." His playful smile returned. "Yes, that was quite a while ago, wasn't it? I haven't played the harp in…" His lips pursed. "Must be near two years now." He waggled his fingers. "They became warrior's hands after all."

A heavy feeling settled into my gut. He'd lost the one thing he'd been so passionate about.

But there was no time for us to mourn the death of childhood dreams. The soldiers still searched for me, and their bellows drew closer as they reached the outskirts of the city.

The boy's smile faded. "Go now," he hissed. "And make haste. I'll try to draw their attention elsewhere, but I can't guarantee they won't search the stream."

He wrapped his arms around my waist, lifting me off the ground and depositing me into the water. I grimaced when the cold liquid sloshed against my raw and still-bleeding feet.

"Here." The boy touched his fingers against my forehead, healing my injuries. "There aren't many stones beneath the water. Once you've reached the river, you can bind stalks of grass to slip over your feet. It will help."

I nodded. But, as I turned, the boy grasped my hand again.

"You never told me your name," he said. His fingers twitched against mine. "I looked for you. Many times. I questioned everyone in the market. But without a name, I had little chance of finding you."

"I have no name," I whispered.

His head tilted sideways. "Surely, you must."

"Terrick," the name tasted like ash on my tongue, "called me lass."

"Lass," the boy repeated. His thumb rubbed my knuckles. "I hope we meet again, Lass."

"And will you tell me your name? Or is this to be a one-sided acquaintance?"

"There's your delightful sarcasm!" he laughed. "Quinn Byrne, at your service." He dipped his head into a small, silly bow.

But the bout of playfulness was short-lived.

"Who's there?" a man shouted. "Oi! There are voices over here!"

"Go," the boy whispered. "Be safe, Lass." He turned and sprinted toward the city.

*Quinn.*

I repeated the name in my head as I trudged through the stream. I didn't want to forget it.

True to Quinn's word, the water never rose above my waist, and its current was gentle. Slow. Easy to navigate. It was frigid, though. A chill seeped into my bones that wouldn't abate, even as the sun rose, bathing the earth in its light and warmth. I continued moving, dragging my heavy feet through the muddy bottom of the water, fighting back the urge to stop, to cry, to wallow in my misery. Quinn had taken a great risk to see me safely from the city. I vowed to reach the river if only to honor the sacrifice he'd made for me.

It was evening again when I found the reverse-swirling current. The waters here were higher, reaching my chest, and more violent. I could go no further.

I climbed up the riverbank, grunting as my hands and feet struggled to find traction on the slick grass. And then I sat there, shivering, as I watched the savagely churning waters.

I wished Quinn had fled with me. Perhaps a few years ago, he would have been eager to escape. We could have run away together, perhaps finding a place where he could practice his music. And I…

Oh, but it was an absurd notion. If Quinn had accompanied me, perhaps he would have found his freedom, but fate would not have been as kind to me. No matter where I went, I carried my power with me. And I'd only ever be seen as a monster.

As darkness descended upon the earth once more, I stood and gave myself another moment to lament everything I'd lost before I walked away.

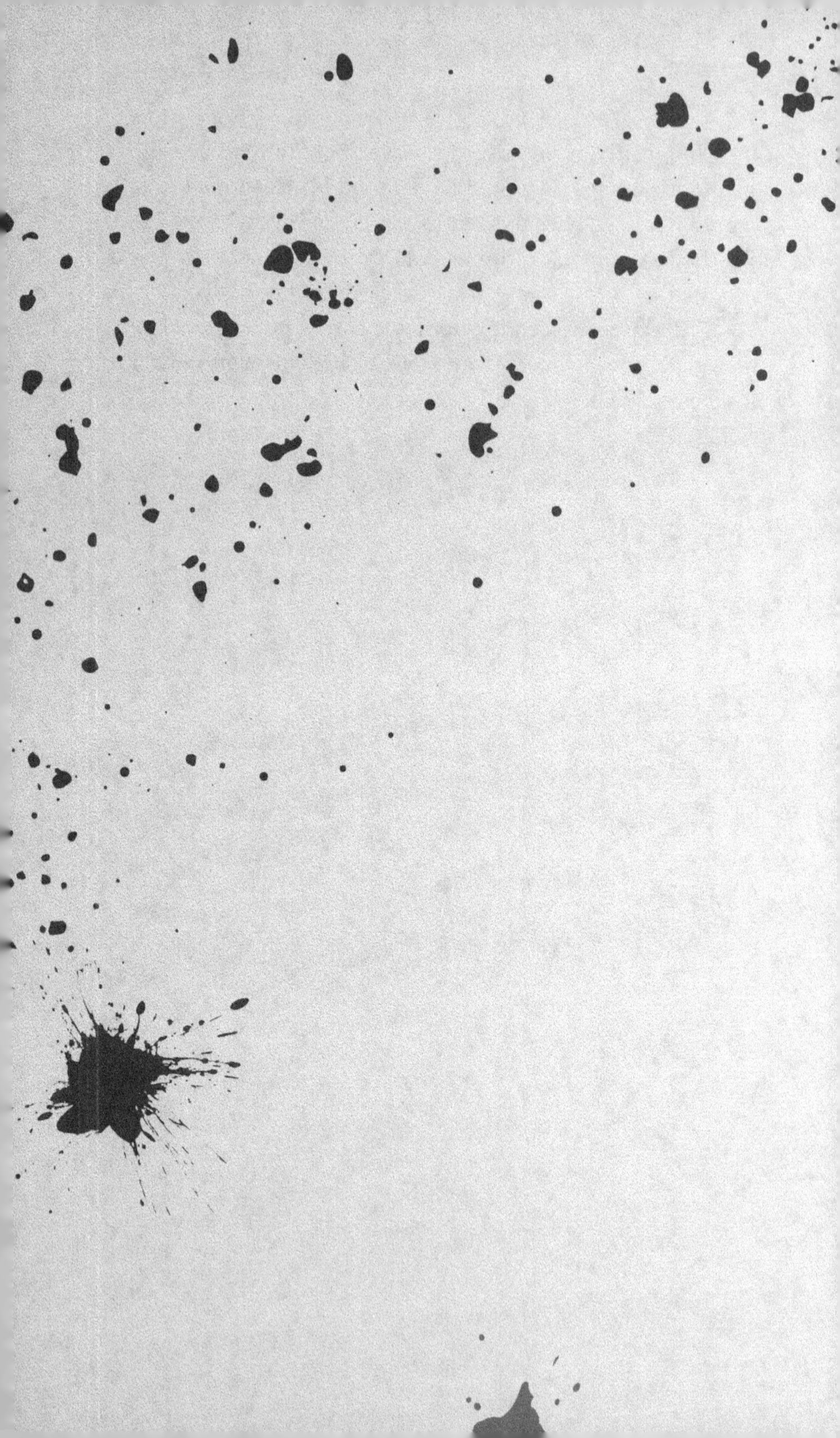

# Polaris

Time is a fickle thing, is it not?

For example: the afternoon sun had still been high in the sky when I began ~~righting~~ writing this tale. But it has long since set, and now the moonlight is decreasing as well. I've sat here for a full day, but it seems as though only mere moments have passed.

I dread what these next days will bring; perhaps another reason time is fleeing from me. I'm worried I won't have enough of it; that I will expire before I ~~right~~ write everything I want to say.

MY YEARS at Darfield had been the opposite: each day so dreadfully tedious that an hour seemed like a year. A year seemed like a decade.

And yet, as I walked along the river and found myself in unfamiliar terrain, my time at Darfield seemed little more than a long night's slumber. The memories of those years were more akin to a dream; too muddled and disorienting to have been real. But those long and very real years had taken a hard toll on me.

A chill seeped into my bones. I trembled so forcefully, my body ached—a deep, gnawing pain that throbbed ~~incessintly~~—incessantly when I was still and wailed when I moved. My feet burned, even though I wrapped them in stalks of grass to protect them from the elements. Walking drove sharp pinpricks of pain into my knees.

The riverbank steepened; the grass slickened. Twice, I nearly slid into the water. After the second time, I cried. I was so cold. The prospect of plunging into the icy water terrified me.

And my tunic was already saturated. I'd started sweating quite profusely, even though I shivered.

"It's not a fever," I said as my teeth chattered.

But it was.

I refused to acknowledge it as I crawled away from the river.

"It's *not* a fever."

Terrick was not here to press cool cloths to my fevered skin, or nurse me through the worst of the illness, as he'd done when he first found me in the woods. A fever would almost certainly mean death.

Perhaps it was what I deserved. But I feared it. My last memories of Mama, with the cough ravaging her lungs and the fever burning her from the inside, were still vivid. Terrifying.

"It's not a fever!"

I dragged myself into the shelter of the nearby forest, certain I would feel warm and steady once I left the eternal chill of the water.

Breathing *hurt*. I became winded after only a few minutes of movement.

I wanted to stop. To lie down.

I was alone, frightened, and weak. But instinct drove me endlessly forward.

Instinct…and Terrick's shadow.

For I heard his voice that day. Clearly. As though he was standing beside me. Guiding me. Protecting me.

*"Find shelter, lass. The weather can turn quicker than a horse rounding cattle. Even if it seems calm, you'll want to make sure you're prepared for the worst."*

"The worst has already happened," I said.

*"It's not so bad as that, lass."* Came Terrick's warm response. *"We'll do it together. Remember what I've taught you."*

Terrick and I had lived in the woods for months before arriving at Swindon. And, upon realizing I did not know the basic skills necessary for surviving in the wild, he had been all too eager to teach me.

Terrick *loved* teaching.

*"Look to the trees. If their branches are thick, they'll shield you from the worst of the wind and rain."*

My knees trembled as I raised my eyes upward. Most trees had shed in preparation for winter, but a great oak still clung to its leaves. They'd turned blood red, and would fall soon, but they'd provide some measure of protection for the night.

*"Well done, lass."*

Though the tree was only a short distance away, it took me several minutes to reach it. I was thoroughly winded as I lowered myself against the expansive trunk.

A leaf fluttered to the ground. For a moment, my fever-addled brain believed the red foliage to be a droplet of blood. I envisioned Terrick's body suspended in the branches above me, blood seeping from his blistered flesh.

I pressed a hand to my churning stomach, fighting back a cry. But when I glanced up, I saw only the branches as they swayed in the breeze, making soft, creaking sounds. It was gentle. And rhythmic. A lullaby.

Through the crimson leaves, I stared at the starry sky. And I remembered the night Terrick and I had lain beneath the moon and stars on a warm summer's eve, a full month before we would arrive at Swindon.

*"Ah, lass," Terrick said, "you see there, the brightest star in the sky?"*

*At the time, I couldn't see what he was pointing at. But I nodded.*

*"That is Polaris," he traced his finger around the constellation. "The Guardian. You'll never be lost, as long as he's watching over you."*

The stars blurred before my teary gaze. But Polaris, hanging high in the sky, still shone more brightly than the rest.

Yet I'd never felt more lost.

My chest ached. For all his faults, Terrick had cared for me. I was certain of that. Everything he'd done in the last years of his life had been to help me.

He'd *loved* me. And I him.

But his love had gotten him killed.

I wished he had never rescued me from the depths of the pond. Drowning may have been an ~~excrutiating~~ excruciating death, but the discomfort would have only lasted a few moments. It certainly would have been less painful than living.

And Terrick would have been free to spend the rest of his days surrounded by his books at Swindon. He could have had many more mornings whistling his happy tune as he strolled to the market. His eventual death would have been peaceful, with the warm touches and well-wishes of friends sending his soul on its final journey.

Instead, he'd spent the last years of his life driven from his home, forced to work a job that took too much from his aging body, and struggling to contain an uncontrollable hybrid.

The fire did not take his life that night. But my presence, my existence, had robbed him of the happiness he'd deserved.

"*I am happy.*" Terrick's warm voice filled my brain once more. "*I'll never leave you, lass.*"

The words were mere memories, but they were all I had left of him.

"*This will pass. Rest. Do not fret.*"

As much as the words comforted me, they also intensified my sorrow.

I sobbed until my throat was raw and it felt as though someone were driving an iron through my skull. All the while, the big oak tree continued to sway above me, singing its mournful lullaby.

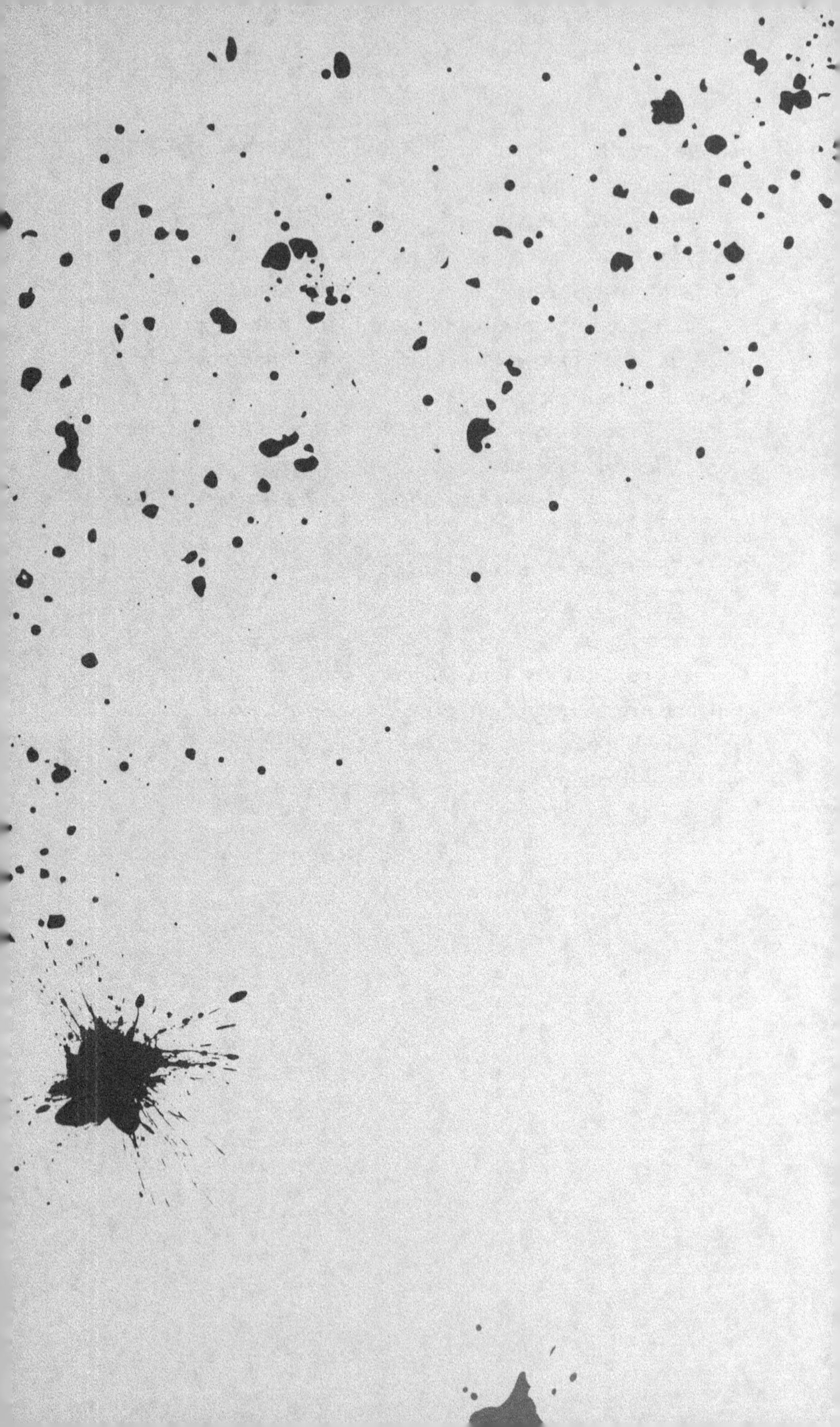

It was the tree that woke me in the wee hours of the morning.

I'm well aware that trees are ~~non-centient~~ non-sentient beings, incapable of thought, rather rational or irrational. But there was, and still is, a part of me that believes the tree had attempted to warn me of approaching danger.

A twig snapped and fell, landing beside my left ear. It sounded like a whiplash in the otherwise quiet wood.

For a moment, while I remained in the disorientating stage between dreaming and waking, I imagined myself back at Detha, listening to the crack of a Wraith's whip. Until I opened my eyes and stared at a foggy sky. The air was cold enough to turn my breath to smoke.

My fever had broken during the night, but my muscles were still raw. My stomach was unsettled—especially when I heard the voices in the wind.

"I 'eard it was Seruf," a man said.

"Seruf?" Another exclaimed. "Have you lost your senses? The message said it was a *child*."

"Aye, but Seurf is quite small, isn' she?"

"How would you know? You've never seen her."

"Old man Rogers has. And 'e swears Seruf is small enough to pass for a child."

"Rogers? That man don't see anything that's not directly under his nose. It's not Seruf, you bloody dolt."

I rose and immediately tensed when my belly sloshed and rumbled.

Leaves crunched underfoot as the men drew closer.

"What if Seruf went and made 'erself a 'ybrid?" one asked.

His companion scoffed.

"And ye think it's only Raphael who's capable of creating 'ybrid?"

"No. But Ramiel and his lot have Wraiths. Why would Seruf weaken her power to give it to a human girl?"

"To trick us," the man said darkly.

I needed to leave.

My legs trembled and the sloshing sensation in my belly made it nearly impossible to move.

~~Salivia~~ saliva filled my mouth as a deep, foul-tasting hiccup rose from my chest.

"Oi! Darragh!" One of the men shouted. "It's 'er."

I glanced over my shoulder. But the men were nowhere to be seen.

"Where?" The second man huffed.

"Ye'll see her in a moment. Quickly. She's workin' up the strength to run."

I bit my lip, swallowed against the increasingly rotten flavor coating my throat, and stood, calling upon my trembling legs to give me all the strength they possessed.

I made it only two steps before I crashed headlong into something solid.

A man suddenly appeared before me.

He was a hybrid—a Traveler, with the ability to dematerialize from one area and re-materialize in another.

According to Terrick, Travelers were rare, and their power took a great toll on their bodies.

This man certainly confirmed Terrick's teachings. He swayed, struggling to keep his feet beneath him.

I turned, hoping his dizziness would give me time to escape, but he grasped the front of my tunic. "It *is* you," he hissed. "This garment is as they described."

There was something cold in the man's golden eyes as they meandered over my body. Something hateful.

"Let me go!" I shouted.

At the same time, the other man's call echoed from behind me. "Left!"

This warning came as I swung my left hand toward my captor.

The golden-eyed man seized my wrist before it connected with his cheek. I stared at him, stunned.

"Do *not* touch 'er hands!" The other man bellowed.

As the words left his mouth, flames danced over my fingertips. The golden-eyed man shifted his hold to my upper arm. "You'll not so easily kill us." His lips curled over his teeth. "Jaxon is a Foreseer."

A Foreseer—one of the rarest hybrids. And one of the most limited, as they saw mere seconds into the future. Nothing more.

If I moved quick enough, perhaps I could ~~thawrt~~ thwart Jaxon's ability…

"Right foot!" Jaxon called.

Again, his words sounded as I lifted my right leg, intending to strike the golden-eyed man's crotch.

The man wasted no time reacting.

I screamed as his mammoth foot crushed mine.

The rancid taste in the back of my mouth grew as my heart made rapid fluttering motions. "Please…" Fire swirled across my knuckles. "Please, I don't want to hurt—"

The man smacked my cheek.

The pain was sudden. And blinding.

"Darragh, no!" Jaxon screamed. "Ye've made it worse!"

Tears stung my eyes. Tears of shock. And hurt. And fear.

Darragh's grip bruised. The fire traveled along my arms, drawing dangerously close to his knuckles…

"I don't want to hurt you!" I whispered.

He drew his other hand back.

I stared at his face, at the vein pulsing in his temple, the look of disgust in his eyes.

"Ye'll need to stun 'er, Darragh!" Jaxon galloped through the trees, breathing heavily.

"Please," I started. "Hel—"

Darragh's fist connected with the side of my head.

Sadly, he was an inadequate fighter. The blow sent a searing pain throughout my skull, but it was misplaced and did little more than daze me.

I vomited, the clear bile spilling down the front of my shirt. My vision swam. I reached for something, anything, to grasp onto.

"Ach, no!" Jaxon called. "Darragh! Don't—"

Darragh cursed as I clutched his tunic. My fire consumed the fabric, singeing his skin.

"—let 'er touch ye." Jaxon's voice was frantic. "She'll kill ye!"

"You monster," Darragh hissed.

His next blow was much more effective.

THE TOWN I was taken to was called Lamex. But it was so similar in size and appearance to Swindon, I at first thought I'd been brought home.

I felt a twinge of excitement as I walked the streets, even as my hands were bound in iron shackles, and chains encircled my ankles. I'd traveled for days like this, hardly able to walk, pushed at a grueling pace anyway. But, for the first time in years, hope blossomed in my chest as I surveyed the town. My head swiveled every which way, trying to absorb my surroundings, hoping I'd find familiar faces amongst the sea of strangers.

But I had no friends in this town.

It was early morning. The streets bustled with market life. Vendors called out prices. Buyers argued the costs were grossly unfair. Children ran and laughed, chasing each other around the shops.

My hands trembled.

I'd been like those children once. Not very long ago.

Jaxon yanked on my chains when I stopped to watch a dark-haired boy share his apple with a bulbous pig. The shackles cut into my raw wrists, and I cried out.

The little boy looked up and startled when he glimpsed my chains. "Mama!" he cried, turning away from the pig and darting to his mother's side.

She'd been deep in consultation with a vendor about a spool of fabric. But she stopped at the sound of her son's distress and drew him against her bosom.

A smug smile stretched across Jaxon's lips. "The boy is wise," he said to me, his voice light and conversational. "'e wanted to come over 'ere to speak with you. I'm glad 'e decided otherwise."

I found myself envious of the boy, wrapped in his mother's loving embrace.

"Don't," Jaxon snarled. "She's no' interested in what ye have to say."

I ignored him. "Please," I whispered to the boy's mother.

Jaxon tugged on my chains.

*"Please!"* I yelled.

A hush fell over the market. Children returned to their parents' sides. Many of the adults gawked at me, looking horror-stricken. But no one reached for a weapon. They did not know me; they hadn't seen my power.

Perhaps I could convince them to spare me kindness…

"Be quiet!" Jaxon hissed in my ear before he straightened and addressed the townspeople directly. "The girl is a prisoner. She may be workin' with Seruf—"

"I am *not*." I tasted salt on my tongue. Tears. "I'm merely a hybrid—"

"*Seruf's* 'ybrid," Jaxon interjected.

*"No, I'm—"*

"The girl killed more than a dozen people in Darfield," Jaxon spoke over me.

"Accidentally!"

"I'll ask that ye give us a wide berth, for yer own safety. We'll be takin' her to Byron, and she'll be dealt with accordingly."

"I'm not a monster!" My chest hollowed as people began vacating the market streets. "I don't want to *hurt* anyone. Please. I'm a hybrid—I don't know how to control—I need *help*."

No one listened.

The hollowness in my chest spread. I supposed I couldn't blame them for their wariness. Had I been in their position, watching a grimy girl beg for help while walking through the streets in chains, I might have chosen caution too.

"Please," I repeated as we continued our trek through the streets. *"Please."*

It would have only taken one person to change the course of my future. One gentle soul to step forward and offer a helping hand. But no one did.

They watched me as we moved toward the center of the town. Their gazes were cold. Frightened.

I stared at my battered, trembling fingers.

"If ye loose yer power here," Jaxon warned. "Ye'll be getting more than a lump on the head. Ye understand? I'd rather keep ye alive, but I'll not hesitate to kill ye if ye hurt anyone." He tapped his thumb against the knife in his belt.

"I can't control it!" I said, for what must have been the umpteenth time.

For the umpteenth time, he ignored me.

"For a Foreseer," I hissed, "there's much you refuse to comprehend."

Jaxon didn't spare me another glance.

Darragh walked behind me, the sharp edge of his sword pressed against my back. He would use it if I stopped again. Darragh had never refused an opportunity to hit me. Indeed, every time the men believed I was at risk of using my powers, I was struck ~~unconcious~~ unconscious. Which was a rather problematic way to travel, considering neither they nor I understood how my power worked.

Jaxon saw too much; too many instances where my power could come to life. He couldn't rely on his foresight to help him. So the men reacted to every noise or movement I made. I'd been struck for sneezing or coughing too loudly—the same infraction my kin at Detha had once been whipped for. I had received a blow to the head when I stubbed my toe on a tree root and had moaned in pain. Another blow had come when I'd swatted a fly that had been biting my ear.

Their harsh treatment was not without consequences.

Throughout our journey, as my head was repeatedly struck, my vision ~~deterated~~ deteriorated. I saw clearly when an object was in front of me. As soon as it shifted to the right or the left, it became fuzzy and unfocused. For example, while walking through Lamex, I could only discern faces if I turned my head and stared directly at them. Otherwise, they were blurred, shadowed shapes in my ~~perhiferal~~ peripheral vision.

It is a disability I still bear. To this day, I still relish the idea of encountering Jaxon and Darragh again and using blunt force to rob their sight. The way they had robbed mine.

Although their harsh treatment paled compared to what awaited me. The leader of Lamex had no plans to shatter my bones or pummel my skull, as my captors had. He sought to destroy my heart, my soul, the very fiber of my being.

And he nearly succeeded.

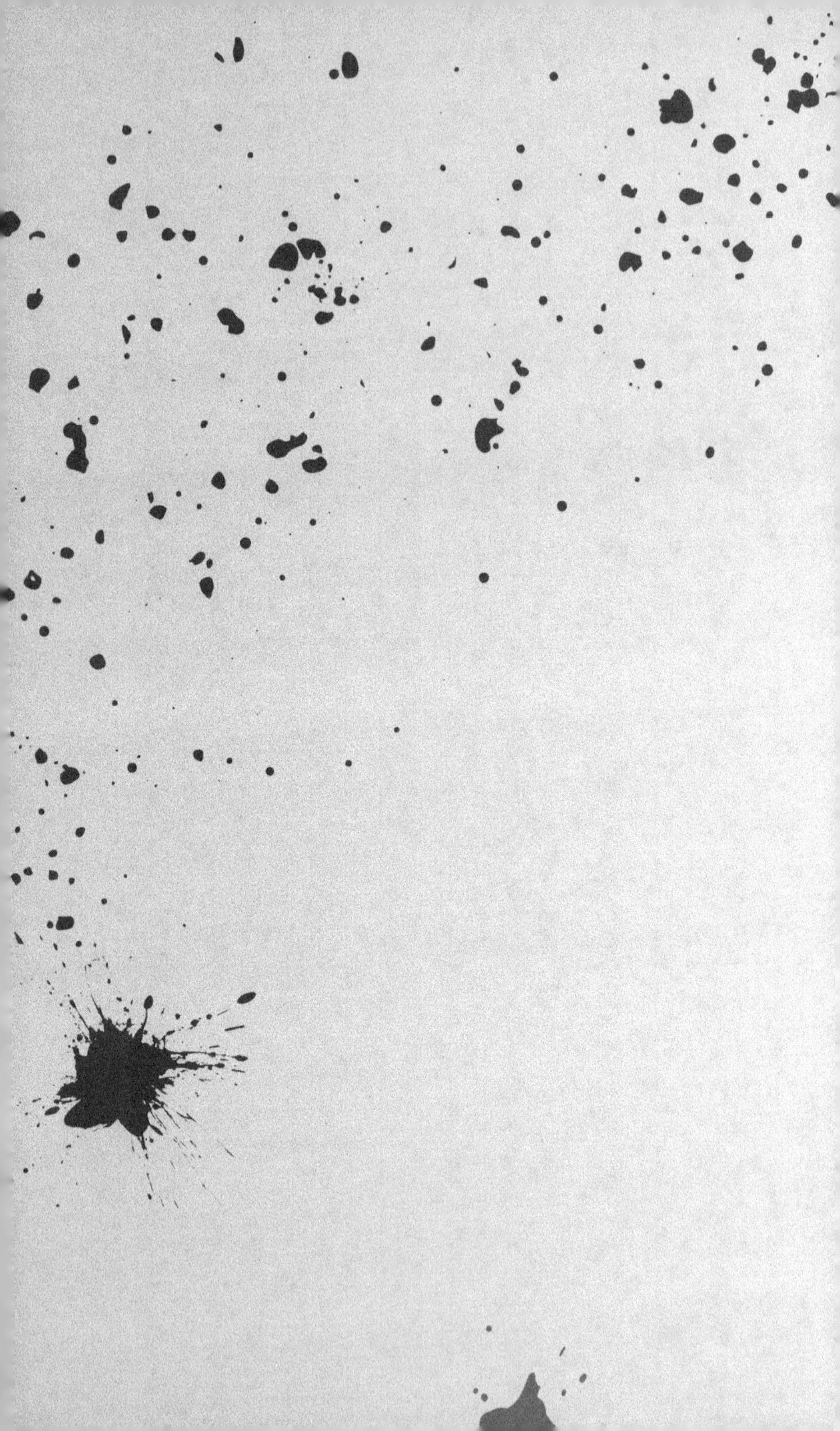

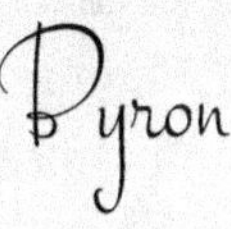

On the edge of Lamex, a sizeable distance from the rest of the buildings, sat a hut. It was small—barely taller than Darragh and Jaxon—circular, windowless, and made entirely of stone.

My stomach curdled as Darragh shoved me through the narrow doorway. A candle sat in the center of the dark room, its miniscule flame casting more shadow than light. But I still saw the shackles nailed to the wall.

"Ah, excellent!" Darragh said gleefully. "So, Alexandra's told him then."

"Aye, well, Speakers have plenty of eyes in the forest, do they no'? *Oi!*" Jaxon shouted when I threw myself backward.

The sight of those shackles gleaming in the otherwise dim room created a strange sensation in my chest. A hollow, yet heart-quickening sense of urgency.

I was too weak to fight against two fully grown men. Darragh's sword pressed into my back. Jaxon yanked on the chains until my wrists screamed in pain. They threw me against the wall, clasping the new shackles in place, ignoring me when I screamed and thrashed.

I was trapped, my hands bound above my head, my feet strapped at an unnatural angle, forcing me to stand on my toes. For the first time, I beseeched my fire to come forth. But when I needed it the most, it had seemingly forsaken me.

"Is this her?" A third man appeared in the room. His deep voice seemed to shake the stone walls of the hut. He stood on my left side. And, as I was pinned to a wall with no room to move, I could not see him. He was simply a blurred figure at the edge of my vision.

"Aye," Jaxon said. "'Twas not easy, to get 'er 'ere alive. She kept trying to attack us—"

"I did *not.*" My lower lip quivered. "You perceived yourself in danger when you weren't and attacked *me* unjustly."

My words went unnoticed.

"And 'tis true, Byron," Jaxon continued. "She is a Firestarter. Like Seruf."

"She almost killed me." Darragh thumped the front of his chest, pointing to his ruined tunic.

"Perhaps if you hadn't struck me, you wouldn't have been burnt," I said.

Again, I was ignored.

"Thank you, Jaxon, Darragh," the blurred figure—Byron—said. "And well done. You may tell Lucia that she's not to take your coin tonight. Whatever you wish to eat or drink will be free of charge."

Jaxon and Darragh exchanged smiles.

Hatred burned inside of me as the men left, celebrating the pain they'd inflicted on another human.

But when Byron moved into my line of sight, my anger shriveled into fear.

Warped and wrinkled burn scars covered much of his face and neck. He was missing his left ear and much of his hair, although a few blonde strands still clung to the right side of his scalp. His nose had melted into disfigurement as well. And his left hand was little more than a gnarled stump.

"Morning," he said cheerily, bouncing on the balls of his feet. "I'd offer a full greeting: *'good'* morning. But I'm not sure that's appropriate. It will not be a pleasant morning for you."

He paced as he spoke, continuously fading in and out of my limited line of sight.

"I'm *not* a Celestial." It took great effort to keep the tremor out of my voice.

"I know." Byron drew his sword, smiling when I flinched, and tapped the edge of the blade against my aching wrists. "You bleed red. Celestials bleed light. No, the claims of you being Seruf are, admittedly, laughable." He resumed his pacing. "I've seen Seruf." He ran a hand over his disfigured chin. "But most have not, so it's hardly a surprise they believed the rumor so easily."

"I am not working for Seruf." I gritted my teeth, trying to ignore the throbbing in my shoulders. "Nor have I ever worked for her."

"Now *that* claim," Byron raised his stump of a hand and pointed it at me, "is much more difficult to confirm."

"It's not," I snarled. "If you'd cease talking and *listen*—"

"You have her power," Byron interrupted.

"I am a hybrid," I said. "No different from any other."

"No different? There are no other hybrids with your power."

"You are merely unaware of their existence." My skin prickled.

"And you've seen others like yourself?" His brow raised. "Give me their names. Their existence will free you from those chains."

I glared at him, but I had no names to give. So I said nothing.

"*Lies.* As I thought." Byron crossed his arms over his chest, surveying me. "What is *your* name?"

"Lass."

"That is not a name."

"It's the only one I have."

"Well, then, Lass," my name sounded like a hiss as it escaped his mouth, "tell me… how did you get your power?"

"The same way other hybrids get theirs."

"You're lying."

"I am not." My palms itched. "I was taken by a Celestial after my mother died. I suffered the transformation and awoke alone."

"Lies."

"My words are only lies because you're *choosing* not to believe them." I wriggled my hands in the shackles, trying to alleviate the itch.

Byron's lip curled. "I'm not interested in listening to you spin a tale, no matter how well fabricated it may be."

"You're not interested in facing the possibility that you may be wrong."

"We have worked too hard, and lost too many lives, ridding Sakar of Ramiel's filth." Byron's jaw ticked. "Seruf was, admittedly, quite intelligent in choosing to send a child into our midst. Too many will forgive a child. Too many will care for one."

I thought of Terrick, my heart sinking. "I am a child no longer," I said. "And you are wrong. No one offered me forgiveness. I was driven out of Swindon and Darfield—"

"Because you murdered innocents."

"*Accidentally.* I can't control it. If you would only *listen*—"

"As you're still young," Byron spoke over me, "perhaps you can still change. And I'd regret not giving you the opportunity to do so."

I yearned to spit in his face. I didn't like the way his colossal frame so easily dwarfed mine, nor how he stared at me; as though I was a disobedient colt who needed to be beaten into submission.

So I spat.

And felt the stinging pain as his palm lashed my cheek.

"That was rude." He wiped my spittle from his chin. "As I was saying, I have no desire to kill a child—no matter how despicable you may be—but I cannot allow you to leave and return to Seruf's side."

"I'm not—"

"So," he continued, his voice dull. Unenthused. "Shall we strike a bargain? If you begin speaking the truth—"

"I have been!"

"—and you tell me of Seruf's plans, I will release you. You'll be permitted to live in Lamex. Under supervision, of course. But it would be a free life. As long as you don't harm others, no one will harm you. You would have my word, as the leader of Lamex."

I swallowed. It was a grossly unfair situation. The idyllic life he described was the only thing I had ever truly wanted. But his promise was empty. That life was a dream.

"Continue lying," Byron's voice brightened, "and in those shackles you will stay. You'll spend the rest of your miserable existence, however long that may be, in this room."

A tremor started in the middle of my back, ~~ricoseting~~ ricocheting along my body. I stared at the dark, windowless room and the scarred man standing before me.

The itch in my palms grew.

"Ah, yes," Byron added, his deformed lips curling into a smile. "I should have mentioned...I had this building specially constructed for your maker." He stroked his scars. "Stone is quite immune to fire, is it not? And those shackles were a gift from the Celestial Ellard. A metal that cannot be melted by flames." He tilted his chin toward my right hand, where a flickering yellow light hovered above my fingertips.

The fire had returned.

But the shackles around my wrists remained cool.

My teeth clicked as the tremors grew. I was no stranger to fear, but the apprehension that festered in my gut as I stared at Byron's gleeful face was unlike anything I'd ever experienced.

Always before, my terror had been at the prospect of hurting others.

Now I feared for myself.

Byron was like a long night in the dead of winter. There was no warmth in him. No light. Only darkness, and bitter cold.

He was a being more akin to Wraiths than humans.

And, once I realized what he could do, I understood why.

"So, what will you choose?" Byron asked.

My voice quivered. "C-considering you won't believe me when I tell the truth, I suppose I'm staying here."

He clapped his hands, delighted. "Very well."

I expected him to use his sword—to slash it against my skin until I was raw and bleeding. Instead, he pressed his fingers against my temple. His hand was hot, his skin ~~callised~~ —calloused. For a moment he stood still, smiling at the fire that danced over my knuckles.

A wave of emotion crashed over me.

Fear.

No, fear is not a strong enough word to describe it. But, alas, I may have difficulty spelling words that would do it justice. ~~Consternation~~ consternation. ~~Trepadation~~ trepidation. *Terror.* The sort of fright that soured one's stomach and turned one's muscles limp. The sort of horror that, embarrassingly, made one lose control of one's bladder and bowels.

My heart felt as though it were being squeezed with an invisible fist.

Byron withdrew his hand as I found the breath to scream.

I slumped in my shackles, my muscles aching, my soul sore and battered.

Byron panted as heavily as I, but he smiled merrily. "Are you sure you'd prefer to stay here?"

I said nothing. My voice had abandoned me.

I didn't understand then what he had done; how he had induced such a hysteria within me. It wasn't until years later that I learned what he was, and had a name to accompany his powers.

Manipulator. A hybrid able to control the emotions of others. Byron could make me experience happiness, peace, fear, anger, hate, love, or anything else he wished me to feel.

Until my creation, Manipulators were considered the rarest hybrids. Only two were made. And their power wreaked havoc upon their minds.

In making me experience such a high level of anxiety, Byron had brought the same fear upon himself. His face paled as he drew a flask from his belt. His hands shook so violently, he had difficulty drinking. Indeed, it took him several tries to remove the cork, and he spilled some of the red wine down his front.

But it seemed he had developed a perverse love for darker emotions. Despite his trembling, he looked full of life and vigor. Whereas I was so feeble, my restraints were the only things keeping me upright.

Byron pushed the cork back into his flask. "Whenever you change your mind, you only need to say so." He stepped toward me again.

I tried to draw back, but I could go nowhere. My head struck the wall.

Byron laughed. "In the meantime, you and I will get to

know each other quite intimately." He pressed his fingers to my temple. This time it was not fear he forced me to experience, but pain. Specifically, the agony of sorrow, of a broken heart.

And, even as I screamed and cried and thrashed against my bindings, I couldn't help thinking: perhaps this was what I deserved.

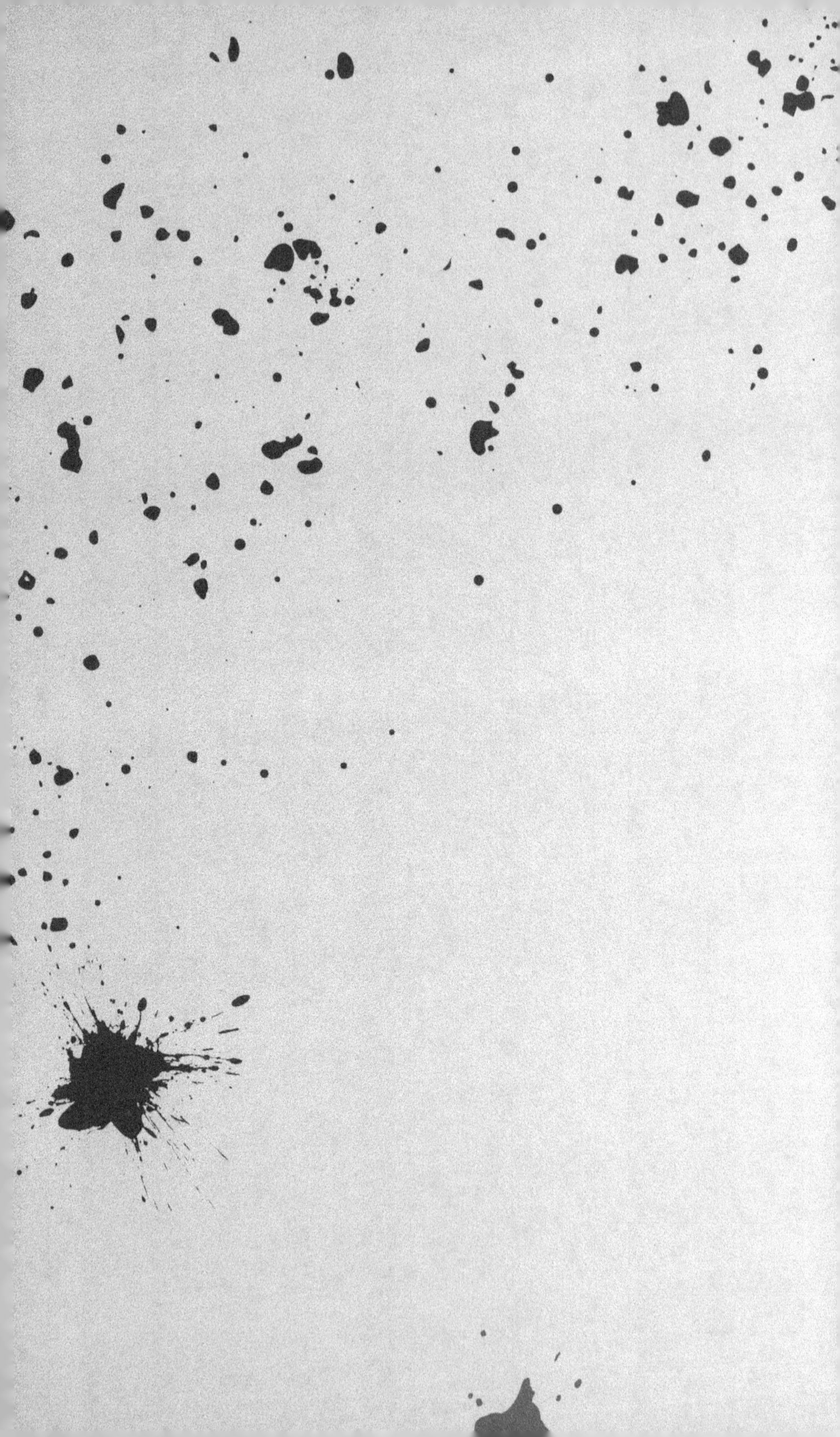

I hung limply in my chains, my arms quivering, wrists aching as the shackles dug into my skin. Tears streamed down my cheeks. No matter how hard I bit my lip or tongue, I couldn't stem the sobs. Byron's doing, of course. My grief was so strong, it was as though he'd physically reached into my chest and crushed my heart.

Then he touched my forehead again, and I was giddy. Full of life and laughter. My muscles yearned to run. To play.

Another touch left a hollow pit in my stomach, my chest once again gnawing with sorrow.

On and on this went. Happiness. Sadness. Happiness. Sadness. Until Byron finally drew away, his hands trembling, his face as pallid as mine surely was.

I sagged, the shackles biting into my wrists, forcing me to stand upright. My legs had grown weary; the muscles in my thighs and calves cramped.

I had toiled in that small, windowless room for several days, unable to move, sit, or lie down.

I was given provisions; scraps of moldy bread and ladles of gritty water that were tossed ~~unceremonsiouly~~ —unceremoniously into my mouth. I choked up more than I swallowed. And, as I could not leave the wall, even to use a privy...well, a body's natural functions couldn't be denied, could they?

So I stood in my own urine, with wedges of barely chewed food coating the front of my tunic, while my emotions withered in utter turmoil.

Byron suffered as well.

He staggered into the wall, his hand quaking so violently, he almost couldn't raise his arm to rap his knuckles against the door.

But he managed. And, at his summon, a woman entered the hut.

She had a round, kind face, and a wild mass of steel gray hair, which she kept twisted in a long braid. She spoke gently to Byron.

"Here you go," she pressed a flask into his palm. "That'll steady your nerves again. Tsk," she clicked her tongue when Bryon raised the flask to his mouth, his unsteady hand spilling much of the wine down his front. "Poor lad." She used the hem of her shirt to clean the mess. "Somedays I swear it's a curse the Celestials left you with."

She turned to look at me. Burn scars wrapped around the left side of her throat. Both her hands also bore puckered blemishes. "It's good work you're doing, Byron." Her eyes held no warmth as she studied me. Only revulsion.

Byron spilled more wine but consumed three large gulps. His shaking quieted. "Is there news from Darfield?" he asked.

"Very little," the woman said. "But there was an attack..." She paused, turning her cold eyes on me again, as though unsure whether to divulge this information in my presence.

Byron did not ask her to continue. He nodded, took another long sip of wine, and straightened. "I am fit to proceed."

The woman nodded, glowered at me once more, and left.

Byron drank from the flask again. And again, before he turned back to me. "What are Seruf's plans?"

I stayed silent.

"Why did she send you?"

I said nothing.

"Why did she create you?"

The only response was my ragged breathing.

"If you would tell me—"

"I can't give you the information you're looking for," I said. "How many times must I explain this?"

"You *won't* give me information."

"There is a difference between 'won't' and 'can't.' Perhaps you should educate yourself on the definition of those words."

His eyes narrowed. "Why do you protect her? It seems she is no longer inclined to protect you. Give me the information I seek, and I will release you from those chains."

He simply wouldn't hear the truth. Unless I fabricated a tale that suited his vendetta, he would ignore anything that came out of my mouth.

So we began the torment again. Sadness. Happiness. Rage. Joy. Despair. This continued for minutes, perhaps hours, the ever-changing emotions twisting my insides until Byron's unsteadiness forced him to stop. Again, he went to the door. Again, the woman brought him more wine and waited until he steadied before she departed.

My head lolled as Byron suckled from his flask. Much of the drink sloshed down his front. The rancid scent of alcohol filled the room and burned my nostrils.

But, oh, how I wished he would offer me a drink. I would have gladly exchanged food for a few sips of wine. The moldy bread did little to ease the niggling pain in my belly, but perhaps the alcohol would have granted me a few moments of sleep.

Instead, I hovered in the foggy area between sleep and waking, unable to fully rest while chained to the wall. I dreamt. Or, rather, my addled brain conjured memories to trick me into thinking I was dreaming.

As Byron slopped his wine, I found myself transported to Terrick's bookshop in Swindon.

*"And this one,"* Terrick's eyes gleamed as he pulled a tome off the shelf, *"has dragons—great winged beasts who breathe fire! Oh, but they're not real, lass." He laughed when I stumbled away.*

*"They're not?" I asked.*

*"No," he said. "They're fiction stories." He waved his arm, gesturing to the ~~colums~~—columns of books and parchments. "They all are. But sometimes the most effective stories contain a grain of truth."*

I was dragged from the fuzzy, albeit pleasant, memory when Byron spoke.

"Wouldn't you prefer to lie down and sleep?" he asked. "Are you not yet tired of those chains?"

*Sometimes the most effective stories contain a grain of truth.*

Could I spin a potent tale around the truth? Would it be enough to end my torment?

Hope fluttered in my battered heart as I willed strength to return to my fatigued body.

"You're a fool," I spat, "if you believe Seruf has lowered herself to confiding in a human."

Byron smiled. "So, you're finally admitting—"

"I know nothing," I said. "But this is my truth. I was born in Detha—"

"Detha?" Byron's red-rimmed eyes widened. He sniffled. "That is in one of the islands of Uchen."

I ignored him, as he'd ignored me these past days. "I became a hybrid and was brought here when I was five—"

"Is that when you began working with Seruf?" his eyes bulged. He reminded me of the fat toad—my first kill.

My palms prickled. Itched. "I was a child. Do you think a cosmic being such as Seruf has the time or desire to rear a child?"

Byron straightened; his nostrils flared. For the first time, he was listening. *Truly* listening.

"I have never interacted with her, as I have said," I continued. "I know nothing of what she is planning, as I have *also* said on numerous occasions. But she created me." The lie rolled easily off my tongue. Perhaps because it wasn't a falsity. It was something I'd suspected for a long while. "Therefore, she must have a plan for me. Perhaps she was waiting for me to come of age. And if such a plan exists, she'll not be happy when she learns of my confinement, will she?"

A flicker of uncertainty crippled Byron's face before he raised his gnarled stump of a hand, gesturing around him. "As you can see, we're amply prepared should she decide to pay a visit to Lamex."

"Amply prepared?" I barked out a laugh. "You have one room and a single set of chains. Tell me, mighty ruler of Lamex, when Seruf comes to save me, how do you propose to contain *two* Firestarters?"

"You're human," he said, although his statement sounded more like a question. "And easy to kill—"

"And ending my life will only incense her further, will it not?"

Byron opened his mouth to speak, but nothing came out.

"I have no wish to harm anyone."

His jaw closed with a snap. "No wish to harm? How can you make such a claim when you've already murdered innocents?"

"*Accidentally.* As I, again, have repeatedly stated. I cannot control my power, but I truly do not wish to harm humans. In fact, I'm quite tired of watching you pathetic creatures die."

Again, my words seemed to have made an impact.

Byron turned away, running his fingers over his scars and staring at the ground as he paced. His breathing grew short and agitated.

He stopped, stared at me, and resumed his pacing. For a moment, he said nothing. Until his mindless wandering brought him back to my side. "Your tunic doesn't burn," he said. "Material from the Celestial city?"

"I don't know. It was a gift from—" My stomach turned to rot as I pictured Terrick's kind smile.

"A Celestial?" Byron supplied.

"No. A friend. Terrick. Perhaps you know of him; he was a hybrid who fought in the war."

"I was a child when that war was fought," Byron said. "Did your *friend* tell you where he got that tunic?"

"He purchased it from a merchant in Darfield."

"Lies."

"No. I invite you to tear a strip of this fabric and take it to Darfield. The merchant displayed this tunic in their window for years and priced it exorbitantly. They were quite proud of it, no matter how they obtained the fabric, and I've no doubt they would verify my claim."

Byron's jaw closed again. He turned away from me, tension roiling across his back. "And what happened to this friend of yours?" he asked. "Why is he not here to defend your innocence?"

"He's dead. *I* killed him."

Byron's jaw twitched, but he turned away, saying nothing.

More tears rolled down my cheeks. I hated the way tears felt; rather like ants crawling across my skin.

For several moments, there was silence, broken only by my grating breaths, and Byron's low, unintelligible murmurs.

His hands ran restlessly over his scars, nails digging into flesh, as though trying to recreate the pain those burns had once inflicted.

I thought of the pockmarked woman who brought him wine. "Seruf has been here before."

Byron remained facing the door. "Yes. A long time ago."

"What did she do to this town?" I asked. "To you?"

"Sakar was not always peaceful. You were not yet born when Ramiel ruled here." Byron gave his scars another vicious scratch.

"I lived the early years of my life in Detha," I said. "I think you'll find I'm well-~~aquainted~~-acquainted with the harshness of a Celestial's rule."

"And Detha is within the borders of Idril—Ramiel's home —is it not?" Byron asked.

"I'm not certain."

"Did you ever see him?"

I had to ponder this; the early years of my childhood seemed like another lifetime. "No," I said. "Only his Wraiths."

"Unsurprising. Ramiel cares little for humans. Some say he finds us revolting. Seruf does not share this view." He turned to face me; his eyes flooded with a dark, raw terror. "You were incorrect in saying Seruf wouldn't have the time or desire to raise a child. Seruf has a *great* desire for children."

He watched me expectantly. As though waiting for me to rebuke or agree with his statement.

When I remained silent, he pivoted and left the room.

I DIDN'T EXPECT him to release me. I was merely hoping for an end—even if it meant him driving his sword through my heart. When Byron returned a day later and began loosening my shackles, I feared I was dreaming.

His eyes were cold as he yanked on the chains with unnecessary force. "I believe you," he said. "You truly do not know Seruf. But I do. She would not have permitted a child to leave her side. Yet, you have never been with her."

"As I've said. *Repeatedly.*" I gasped as blood returned to the fingers of my newly freed arm. It felt as though there were spikes inside me, clawing at my skin.

Byron wrenched my other arm away from the wall. "Your separation from Seruf was likely a mistake. And it seems she has returned to Sakar to remedy it."

I winced when he tossed the chain away from my left wrist, sending the heavy metal slamming into my side.

"Against my better judgment," his lips curled over his teeth, "I'm setting you free, but you cannot stay here. I'd advise you to enjoy your liberation. It's not likely to last long."

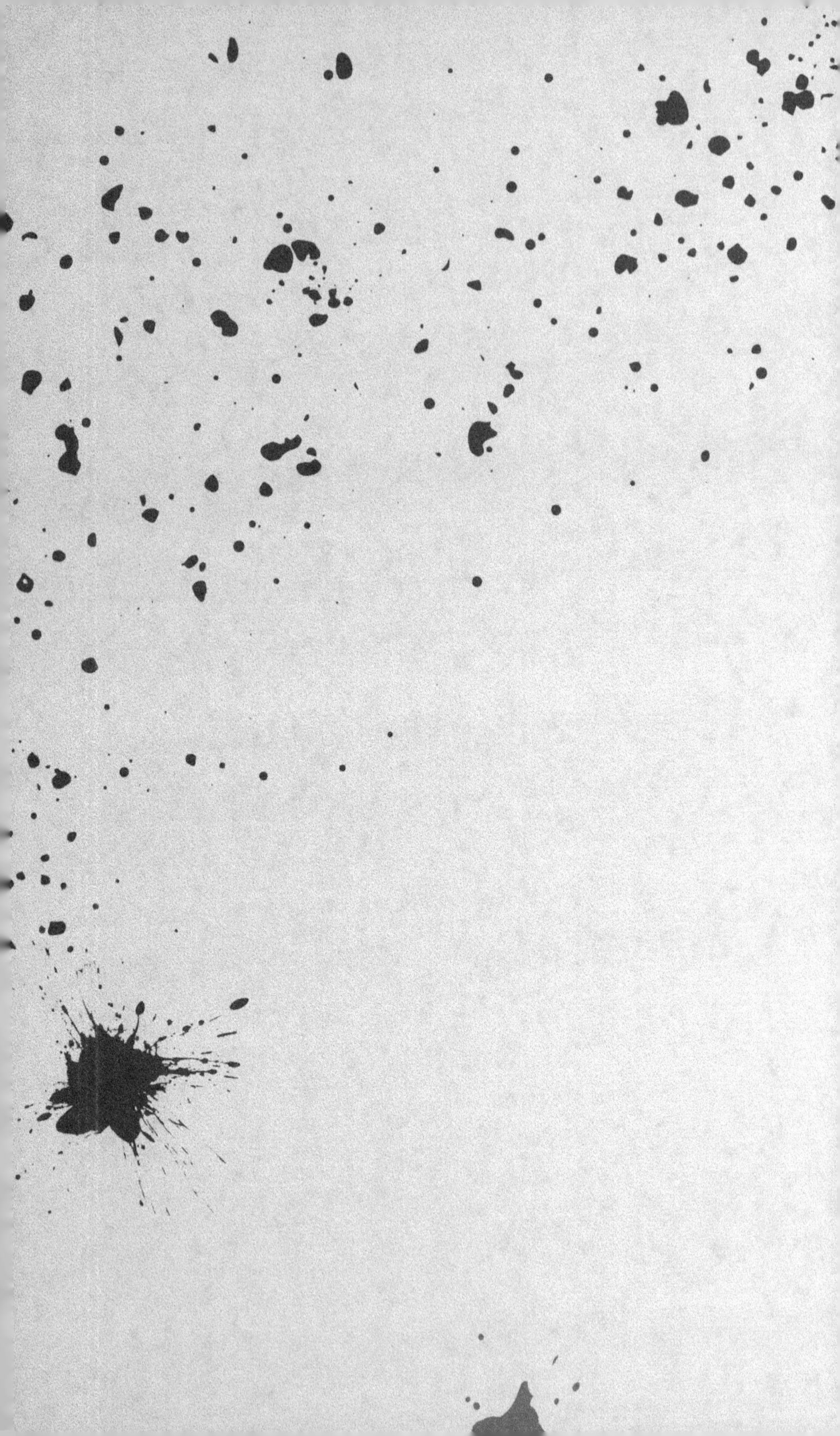

# Run

Darragh and Jaxon returned to escort me out of Lamex. I saw them for only a moment, staring at me in repulsion, before Byron pulled a burlap sack over my head.

"Take her into the forest," Byron instructed as he tied a rope around my hands.

"How far?" Jaxon asked.

Byron tugged at my arms when I reached for the sack, attempting to free my mouth. "You'll leave that on if you want to stay ~~concious~~ conscious," he hissed before saying to the men, "One day's walk. Be sure she doesn't know how to return to Lamex."

"And if she looses 'er power?"

"Do what you must to ensure she doesn't."

For twenty-four hours, we walked. Jaxon, again, held my bound hands. Darragh kept a sword pressed to my back. Neither spoke, and their tension seemed palpable.

"This should be far enough," Darragh said after the long stretch of silence.

The sound of his voice startled me.

"Ach." Jaxon, mistaking my flinch for an attempt to flee,

jerked on the rope. "No, ye don'. Ye'll be free to go soon, mind, but we'll no' have you followin' us through the forest."

The rope around my wrists tightened with a painful snap. My knuckles scraped against hard tree bark.

"Ye'll have to untie yerself," Jaxon said. "Or simply use yer power and burn the rope away. But know ye'll be noticed, and hunted, if ye destroy the forest."

They left me tied to a branch of that birch tree.

And, as my wretched flame never appeared when I most needed its help, it took more than an hour of fiddling to undo the knot.

I was left with a three-day ration of food and water. Nothing else. No weapons to hunt with, no additional clothing. Not even a pair of boots.

Thus, I walked.

I had no destination in mind; merely the notion that moving was preferable to standing still.

And I was hunted.

Even when I delved deep into the forest, where the thicket of barren trees barred the sun from casting its light upon the ground, soldiers relentlessly pursued me.

I LAY flat on my belly, hidden beneath a bush, while two women roamed the clearing.

"Byron's a fool," one said as she knelt to inspect the ground. Looking for my footprints, no doubt.

Fortunately, my bare feet left shallow impressions that were quite easy to cover up.

"He fears Seruf," the other woman commented. "And did not want to bring her wrath upon his people." Her fingers cast a luminous glow in the dark wood. She was a hybrid—an Illuminator.

The light tore at her skin, creating shallow fissures that oozed blood. But she did not allow her power to dim as she searched through the tree branches.

I flattened myself to the ground, burying my nose into the soft soil, struggling to keep my breathing even and slow.

"But he had her *contained*," the first woman spat in disgust. "If he'd *questioned* her, perhaps he would have found a weakness—"

"We do not yet know the connection between Seruf and her pet." The Illuminator's light seeped through the foliage. "Likely Byron thought freeing the girl would draw Seruf's gaze away from Lamex. Perhaps he chose the right course of action, perhaps not. Time will tell. I only hope the girl is found before—"

The light pierced my bush, nearly blinding me. But my whimper of fear was suppressed by the Illuminator's cry of triumph.

"She's here!" The Illuminator tore through the spindly branches of the bush and grasped my tunic. She dragged me across the ground, ignoring me when I yelled and thrashed and pleaded.

"Cara!" She called to her companion. "Hurry!"

My skin prickled. The ~~salivia~~ saliva evaporated from my tongue. "Don't do this!" I begged. "Please!" The itch grew sharper. Burning. Maddening. As it always was before the flames emerged. "I don't want to hurt—"

But it was too late.

As the other woman rushed forward, her sword raised over her head, my skin burst into flames. The more I writhed, desperate to distance myself from the women, the more incensed my fire became.

My flailing arms brushed a strand of the Illuminator's

dark hair. She howled as the flame latched on, spreading across her scalp and down her face. The other woman faltered, lowered her sword, and rushed to her companion's aid.

"Leave me!" The Illuminator wailed. Her skin bubbled. The sulfuric scent of burnt hair filled the air. "Get the *girl!*"

My fire roared across the ground, ~~ravenisly~~ ravenously devouring everything in its path.

Including the two women.

In the aftermath, I sat beside their smoldering remains, shaking. The fire had long abandoned me, but it still pulsed through my veins. Impatiently awaiting its next meal.

Men and women continued to roam the woods, searching for me. The Firestarter, I'd been dubbed. The *"girl wearing a Celestial's garment."*

As my beautiful, shimmering tunic did not blend with the colors of the forest, I rid myself of it. Burying it, because I could not bring myself to destroy it.

It pained me to throw dirt over the beautiful fabric; Terrick's gift to me. The only thing I had left of him.

I stared at the swaying trees encircling the tunic's resting place. "Guard this for me. Please," I beseeched them. "Keep its location hidden. Safe. I'll come back for it one day."

I memorized the clearing, and the path I took away from it, fully intending to return.

But I never did.

Of course, burying the tunic may have helped conceal me from my hunters, but it further exposed me to the elements. Thankfully, the weather remained mild; winter had not yet taken a firm hold of the land. But insects feasted on my blood and left painful welts all over my body. Some plants were coated in poisons that left me covered from head to toe in hives.

*"Look at the* leaves, *lass,"* the memory of Terrick's voice gently chided. *"The ones that shine or grow in clusters of three mean you harm."*

I'd forgotten much of his teachings. I'd been so young when we spent that summer in the woods. The memories had mostly faded, but they began to trickle back as I navigated the forest, desperately evading my captors.

Days passed in a slow trickle.

And my hunters were never far away.

"So you 'eard the story from Charlie, who 'eard it from Lola—who 'appens to be a scandalmonger, mind," One man called out as he stood beside the fallen log I'd burrowed myself into. Quite an ingenious hiding spot: the thick oak wood concealed me. I'd only be discovered if a person dropped to their hands and knees and peered into the shallow opening, which was partially submerged in a muddy puddle.

The unfortunate aspect of being so close to a pool of stagnant water were the bugs. Small insects hummed ~~incessintly~~ —incessantly around my ear. And this man, so intoxicated he could no longer speak without slurring, had decided the puddle was a perfect location to defecate. The putrid odor rising from his feces made my eyes tear.

His companion, too far away for me to hear clearly, responded.

The man beside my log laughed. Rather perfect timing, as my stomach chose that moment to give a tremendous heave in protest of the stench. But my soft, dry gag went unnoticed.

*"You can drink fresh, running water, lass."* Terrick's voice

*echoed in my mind. "But the water from a stagnant pond will make you ill."*

I'd never fully comprehended how revolting a stagnant body of water was until that moment. For there were no waves or currents to remove the feces. It merely stayed where it landed, festering, and contaminating everything around it.

"Has Seruf truly arrived in Sakar?" the man asked, still chuckling. "Or is Lola merely spreading 'er rumors?"

The conversation from that point onward centered on Lola, and the way she used her plentiful bosom when she wanted to beguile soldiers into giving her information. There was quite a bit of talk of her bosom. At least until the man finished spewing his toxic odors and stood, pulling his trousers over his hips.

I saw his knife fall, and I stopped breathing as it landed with a *plop* in the murky water.

"For feck's sake!" the man knelt to retrieve his blade. His eyes flashed as he caught sight of me, huddled in the log. "You bloody—" he snatched my legs. "Hiding now, are you? Waiting for—*oof.*"

I swung my arm, my knuckles catching the side of his throat, winding him. As he wheezed, I slithered out of the log, landing in the water with a splash.

*Water.* I gasped in relief. The itch rippled across my skin as the fire thundered in my veins. But it did not emerge. It couldn't. Not while I was submerged.

"You fecking *bitch!*" The man seized a fistful of my hair, dragging me out of the puddle.

"Stop!" I clawed at his hands. "Leave me in the water!"

The man shoved me backward onto the ground and wrapped a lock of my hair around his fist. "Hmmph," he grunted as he twisted my neck back. "They didn' say you was pretty."

I disliked the hungry look in his eyes as he gazed upon my bare flesh.

His hand stretched toward my chest. "If ye can keep that power of yours contained for five minutes, I'll let you leave. Ten minutes, and I'll hide your trail." He winked.

His ~~callis~~ callous-roughened hands hurt when they touched my skin. His breath smelled of ale and decay.

The fire inside me roared.

*"Remember, lass,"* Terrick said, *"When you hunt, be sure to kill the animal quickly. If your initial wound wasn't fatal, find the beast and end its misery. There's no need for any creature to suffer."*

I burst free of the man's hold and grasped his face in my flame-wrapped hands. And I felt no remorse when he cursed and bawled. Instead, the sounds incensed me to keep clutching onto him until he perished.

A quick death. As Terrick had taught me.

There was also no shame in me when I repeated my actions with the man's equally odious companion.

*So this is to be my fate,* I thought glumly in the aftermath.

To be hunted. To kill those who wished to kill me. And to repeat the horrendous process each day until I perished.

THE NEXT DAY, I took shelter inside a yawning tree hollow as yet another group of hunters approached.

"It took Seruf a mere *hour* to breach Darfield's borders." A boy said in a hushed whisper as the soldiers rode their horses past my tree.

*Darfield.*

I trembled as I pressed myself to the back of the tree trunk.

"How?" A woman asked. "Darfield has one of the largest hybrid armies in Sakar. *And* the protection of a Celestial."

"Aye. Maya said Ellard Fell," the boy said grimly.

Another woman gasped. "Is she certain?"

"She seemed to be."

"It—but—how is that possible? Without Ramiel—"

"Who's to say he's not accompanying Seruf? Even if he's not been seen yet," the boy said. "And with Seruf's hybrid on the rampage…"

I could barely hear the next words over my booming heart.

"We need to find that hybrid," the woman snapped. "Before she kills us."

But they didn't find me. Not that day.

My stomach soured as the riders continued their trek, and the nausea persisted even after they'd disappeared.

*Darfield.* It wasn't a coincidence Seruf had attacked my old home.

I wondered what had happened to the blue-eyed boy. Quinn. Had he perished in battle?

Tears filled my eyes. I hope he had—a quick, painless death. For that was preferable to being turned into a Wraith, the fate that surely awaited any living soldier defeated by Seruf's army.

MORE DAYS PASSED. The cooling autumn breeze carried whispers of pain. And fear. The animals must have sensed it too. Birds stayed closer to their nests, no longer singing their morning tunes. Rodents scurried to safety, only emerging to gather food. Squirrels huddled in the trees. Deer traveled in tightly knit groups. Even the predators seemed reluctant to emerge from their dens and hunt.

On some afternoons, the sound of my bare feet shuffling through the leaves seemed deafeningly loud in the quiet woods.

A chill seeped into my bones. A deep, bitter cold. Accompanied by a pain I knew well.

Fever. Hardly a surprise, given the recent torment my body had endured.

Walking became a tremendous struggle. Each step was ~~monumentous~~ momentous, as though I were climbing a mountain, rather than trekking across mostly flat terrain. My vision worsened; even objects directly in front of me seemed unfocused. Breathing brought a sharp, stabbing pain to my lungs.

Soon, that pain turned liquidy (is this a word? Liquidy— *watery?*), as though someone had filled my chest with molten metal.

I began coughing.

The fits hit suddenly, with little warning, and often left me doubled over, struggling to inhale.

Still, I moved forward, choking on great mouthfuls of blood and mucus. The ~~flem~~ (goodness, is this a word? I believe it is). ~~Phlem~~ Phlegm filled my throat and airways, making it impossible for me to take a breath. And when air wormed into my lungs, it rattled the hot liquid inside my chest and created another fit.

My ailing body could go no further.

And that afternoon, as I lay shivering, despite the relative warmth of the day, my arduous journey ended.

Rough fingers clasped my shoulders. Metal coiled around my wrist. Hands scraped at my raw skin as I was flung into a saddle.

"If you burn my horse," a woman warmed me as she settled herself into the saddle behind me, "or *me,* I will slit your throat. Do you understand?"

I nodded as I stared at the horse's gray mane. "I don't want to hurt people."

The woman made a sound of disbelief.

"Truly. I-I—have you ever lost control of your stallion?" I asked. The horse's muscles quivered beneath me. He fidgeted and ground his teeth against his bit. All signs of a high-spirited animal. And given his impressive height and strong legs, I imagined he was a powerful runner.

"Javen is well trained," the woman said.

"Perhaps now," I said. "He wasn't always. I'm certain he's taken you—perhaps merely at a faster pace than you expected."

"Of course." The woman tightened the reins when the horse began bobbing his head in earnest.

"Then you're well-aquainted—acquainted with the sensation of having a beast that is both larger and stronger than you take any illusion of control you thought you had. That is how I feel when my wretched power surfaces." Tears sidled down my cheeks. "It is an unbridled stallion, wreaking havoc as it thunders through the land. And I am a rider, strapped to its back without the means to halt it. I've no wish to hurt people. But I cannot stop myself from doing so." I turned, although the woman remained a blurred figure on the outskirts of my damaged vision. "Kill me. Please. It's the only way to guarantee I won't harm anyone else."

"If it were up to me, I'd bleed you out here and now. You're a wretched creature who doesn't deserve to draw breath. But," the woman clicked her tongue and shifted her legs, urging the stallion into a trot, "we need answers about your master."

So I was to be tortured. Again.

The thought did not fill me with fear or dread. It only left me exhausted. "You're making a mistake," I whispered.

Of course, I didn't know the full gravity of that mistake. Not until several days later.

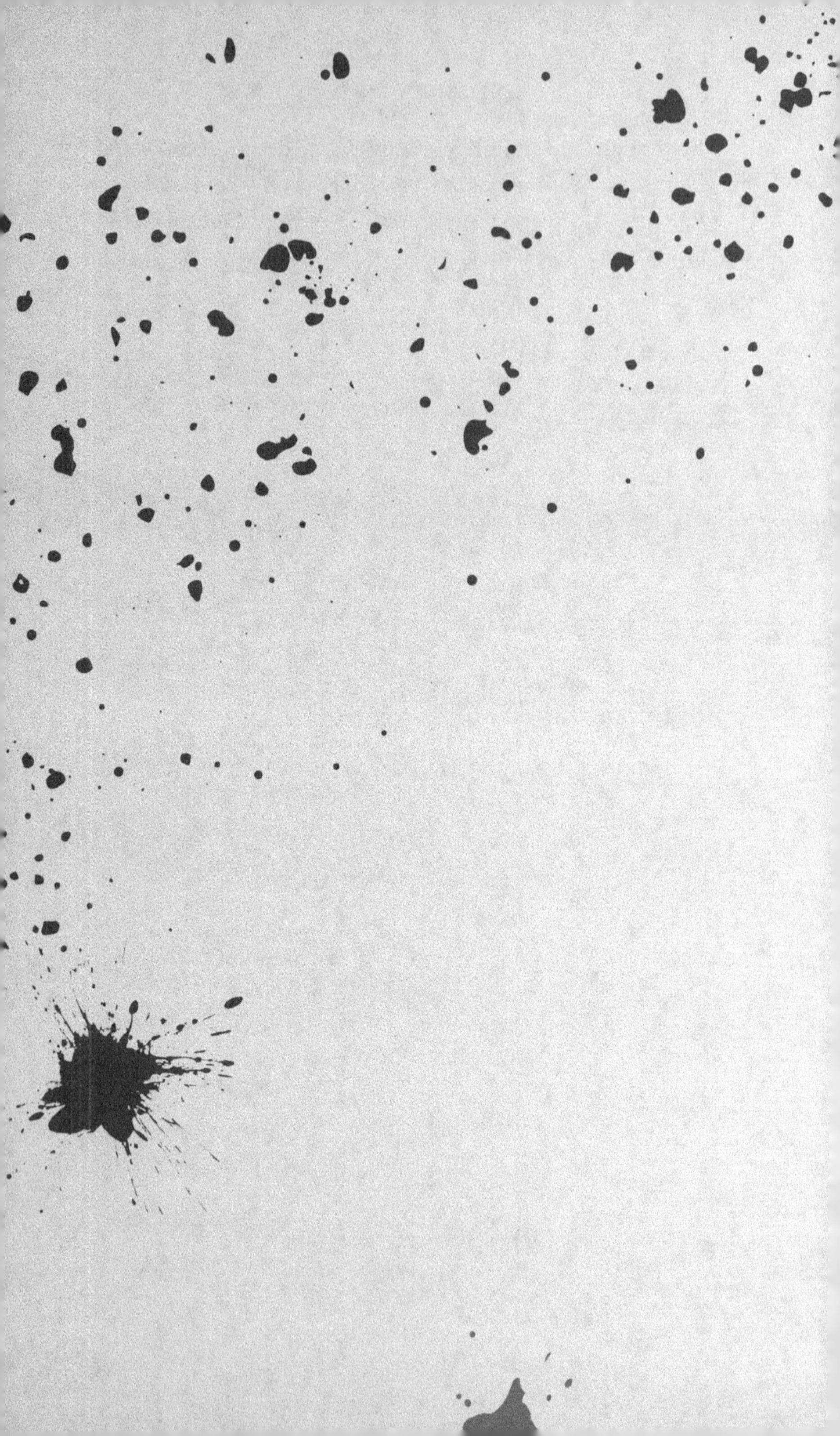

# Vaporia

I was dreaming.

I stood in a smoldering city. Billowing clouds of smoke hung over the houses. The wind caressed my cheek, bringing with it the smell of ash and incinerated flesh. The scent of death.

These streets were unfamiliar, as was the majestic white castle that stood gallantly in the distance. Yet they *seemed* familiar, as though I'd visited this place before. Perhaps in another dream.

A woman stood before me, her golden hair cascading over her shoulder. I never glimpsed her face, as she kept her back toward me, but I approached her gleefully. As though she were an old friend, one I was intimately ~~aquainted~~ acquainted with.

This woman was a stranger.

Yet I was so excited at the prospect of seeing her, of speaking with her, that I sprinted the last few steps. Her name rested on the tip of my tongue—and I was certain it was her name, even if I'd never uttered the word before.

The wind blew again, harsher this time.

The golden-haired woman vanished.

But the odor of smoke and death only intensified. And soon the familiar sound of wailing accompanied it.

I lurched forward, crying out when I found myself falling, my body plummeting for what seemed like an eternity before I hit the ground.

Above me, a horse snorted, and the echoing sound of hooves against hard dirt struck close to my ear. The animal had very nearly trampled me.

Such a shame it missed.

"The girl!" Someone called, although their voice seemed far away. "The bloody horse ran off!"

I wrenched my eyes open and coughed, spitting out a mouthful of dirt. It took several tries to lift myself off the ground—my hands were bound, and my muscles weak. The change in height as I went from lying to sitting left me winded.

Smoke curled through the air. Heavy, black smoke, too thick to see through.

I squinted, a sliver of fear striking my gut.

I'd lost control of my power again, hadn't I?

The surrounding shrieks deafened me but I saw nothing through the plume. I didn't know how many people were suffering. Hundreds, perhaps thousands.

My stomach ached. Would the fire ever be satiated? Even my fever hadn't dampened its appetite.

A shadow caught my eye, and I turned as a woman staggered into me.

My heart leapt and I wondered—*hoped*—if this was the golden-haired woman from my dream. But sadly, 'twas not. This woman had a mane of dark hair. I recognized her.

My captor.

I'd spent the last three days riding with her as I drifted in and out of ~~consiousness~~ ~~conciou~~ consciousness. Every time I woke, she threatened to kill me.

"If I see but a wisp of smoke," she had snarled, many times, "I won't hesitate." She punctuated her words by pressing the flat side of a steel blade to my throat. Even while riding on a briskly jogging horse and holding my prone body steady with her right arm, it took her a mere second to draw her knife.

Of course, when I asked her to follow through with her warnings, she refused. "We need you alive. But *I* want you to feel the pain you've inflicted on others." And then she would dig the edge of the blade into my neck, my shoulders, or my arms. The shallow cuts drew blood but were not enough to end my life.

I was, after all, labeled as Seruf's pet. An evil, inhuman monster that needed to suffer.

And now this woman, who'd once happily lashed at my skin, grasped onto my shoulders, her eyes wild with fear. She breathed almost as poorly as I—her every inhale a long wheeze.

"You should have killed me," I told her.

"What?"

"You should have killed me!" A salty tear splashed across my lips. "You buffoons simply won't *listen*. You insist on keeping me alive, threatening death, but failing to deliver it."

"What are you blathering about?" she snapped.

I gestured wildly to the vapors surrounding us. "How many times must I repeat myself? I *cannot* control my power!" Yelling made my lungs burn, so I quieted my voice. "Killing me won't save this place, but it will prevent this from happening again. Stop making empty promises and *do it*."

The woman opened her mouth but paused as the screams swelled around us. The noise seemed almost tangible; as though I could stretch out my hand and physically grasp a person's pain.

"This wasn't you," the woman said.

Surprisingly, her words did not bring relief. "It wasn't?"

"No. This is Seruf's work." Unshed tears made the woman's eyes glisten. "Vaporia's streets were ablaze before we crossed its borders. You didn't do this. But you do not burn. And you claim you are innocent. If you've no wish to harm people, *help* them." She knelt before me. The wind blew her hair across her face, causing several strands to stick to her tear-streaked cheeks. "The citizens of Vaporia are dying; many are trapped inside their homes. The fire spread too quickly. There was no time for them to evacuate. But you *don't burn!* You can save some of them. Prove your innocence," she whispered, "and I'll free you."

Truthfully, it was tempting to use my ability for something good. Perhaps the act of valor would have eased some of the guilt I'd been carrying with me.

Perhaps not.

Saving a life wouldn't change the fact that I'd taken lives. Many of them.

"And if I were to lose control, what then?" I fought to steady my voice. "Will you kill me? Or continue to make empty threats?"

She swallowed. "Well, you could hardly do more damage—"

"I certainly could." A bitter sensation coiled in my chest. "Some may yet have a chance to escape and live. I can ensure no one survives."

The woman's breath hitched. "You would damn them all to die?"

"You would have damned me to a fate far worse." My vision grew so blurry, the woman was reduced to little more than a shadow. "You used me as a scapegoat, an outlet for your own fears and shortcomings. You've hunted me. Tortured me. Despised me." I wiped the moisture from my eyes. "And now you want me to show compassion for people who would have gladly seen me suffer? I will not. I have *never* worked for Seruf. But I will not protect you from her wrath."

"You insolent wench!" The woman reached for her knife.

"Kill me. I'm begging you to," I taunted.

She paused, shaking her head. "No. I will not grant you that wish. I'd rather you *suffer*."

"Then leave me." I shrugged. "Or stay if you'll not be satisfied until you see me in pain. But I, as you already pointed out, will not burn in this inferno. You will."

She stood and stepped back, her eyes roaming around the towering flames encircling us.

"You all wished me to be a monster," I said. "And I'm tired of trying to convince you I'm not. So a monster I shall be."

A gust of wind caused glittering embers to rain down upon us. The cinders evaporated off my skin but left welts on the woman's exposed flesh.

She gave me one long, frightened look before she ran.

Her sudden departure wasn't a surprise. Death by fire is one of the most ~~excrutiating~~ excruciating ways to perish. Or so I've been told.

Perhaps I'd been foolish in letting my anger best me. Perhaps the woman would have upheld her end of the bargain and granted me ~~leinceny~~ leniency if I'd saved some of the townsfolk.

Even if she had, my freedom would've been short-lived. Because humans never changed. They feared what they didn't understand, and that fear drove them to cruelty.

My life stretched before me as an endless cycle. I would live in peace, for a time. But the fire would take control again.

It would kill again. And I would be hunted. Until someone else made an offer of peace and began the cycle over.

I was tired of traveling around that eternal loop.

So I made it stop.

And I felt nothing as I listened to the people of Vaporia die.

Perhaps my body was too weary to process emotions. Or, perhaps, their accusations had been right, and I'd never been fully human. I was merely a creature with fire in my veins and a heart made of coal.

I sat, listening to their cries, their shouts, their pleas, and I watched as the fire crept ever closer to me.

Flames can be quite tranquil, can they not?

I'd never noticed before because I'd always regarded them with terror. But, as I sat there, in the middle of a dying village, I found peace. There was something soothing in the scintillating light. The smoke billowing around me seemed to be a healing balm. The more I inhaled it, the less my chest ached.

Time slid away. I might've sat there for moments, or hours. Or longer.

The wails of the dying faded. The crackling hiss of smoldering wood rose.

I tucked my legs into my chest as the flames drew ever closer, bathing my feverish skin in a glorious heat. I stretched my hands forward, desperate to feel more of its warmth.

The last time I'd reached for a flame, I'd been a child.

*"You must never go too close to a fire, love,"* Mama had said as she placed a damp cloth over my burnt hand.

The scars from that day were still visible; small circles of puckered flesh on the tips of my pointer and index fingers.

Now, of course, the flames danced merrily over my skin, leaving me unscathed.

What would Mama have thought of me, if she'd lived long enough to see me become what I was? Would she have still loved me, despite the lives I'd taken? Or would she have turned on me, as everyone else had?

"Child."

The voice that spoke to me was gentle. But the smoke was now so thick, I could barely see the tip of my own nose. I certainly could not discern the speaker amongst the heavy clouds.

Anger coiled again. Had I not made it clear I wanted to be left alone? "As I've explained already," I snarled, "I will not save you from Seruf's fire. Your time would be best spent escaping the city. If you can."

A soft chuckle swirled around me. "Oh, my child, I have no wish for you to rescue the humans. You wouldn't be able to anyway. There is no one left to save."

Unease unfurled along my spine. The speaker was too calm—her voice filled with too much mirth. "Who are you?" I asked.

She didn't respond immediately. Instead, the smoke dissipated, as though it had been commanded to retreat. The swirls thinned, allowing me to glimpse the woman standing before me.

Except she *wasn't* a woman.

Two ~~volumous~~ voluminous black and red wings cascaded down her back, the feathers shimmering like a liquid pool. She wore a magnificent gown made of a silver material that radiated through the darkness. Her teeth, when she smiled, were rather unnatural—far too white and straight.

Something cold and dark grasped my insides. I did not need her to introduce herself. I knew who she was. "Seruf," I said.

"Indeed." She smiled as she surveyed my bare, unburnt skin. "My dear child…I thought I'd never see you again."

# Seruf

The vague childhood memories I had of Seruf were faded and distorted. I'd long envisioned her as a winged Wraith: warped and inhuman. A horrifying sight to behold.

But Seruf was merely a winged woman. She seemed unthreatening. Especially as she stared at me, her dark eyes gleaming with joy and relief.

I did not fear her. Truthfully, I did not seem capable of feeling *anything*. My heart churned away inside my chest, but it had turned into something resembling a clockwork mechanism, like in Terrick's fiction books. A device that mimicked life but was incapable of truly living.

"My child." Seruf folded her knees into a crouch as she surveyed me. "What have they done to you?"

I stared at her but said nothing.

Around us, the smoke continued to clear, revealing rows upon rows of debris-covered streets. Burnt remnants of humans and beasts crisscrossed along the road. This had been a rather large town, once, if the ruins were any indication. Easily twice the size of Swindon, and likely housing twice the number of humans.

Those humans were all dead.

I wanted to pity them. But I didn't.

"I heard you had returned to Sakar," I said to Seruf.

She beamed at me. "For you," she said. "I returned for *you*."

"So it's true." My stomach turned hollow. "The accusations—"

"Accusations?"

"That I was created by your hand."

"Ah," Seruf's smile stretched, if possible, even wider. She looked rather comical, with her too-white teeth glinting in the dying fire. "Of course it's true." She raised her hand. The tips of her fingers (the nails, to be more accurate) were painted a dark shade of red.

It looked as though she'd dipped them in blood.

She shifted her fingers and summoned a tongue of fire. It hovered, still and quiet, above her palm.

She closed her fist, extinguishing the flame.

I envied how easily she accomplished that. How many times had I fought to banish the fire from my skin? How many times had I lost control over it? And yet, she made controlling it seem as simple as…well, as closing her fist.

"I am the last fire elemental to live in this wretched place. My brethren sided with Raphael," Seruf said. "Imagine that. We were bonded; closer than—well, there isn't a human equivalent to describe what we were to each other. Closer than kin, certainly. And yet they *left* me."

"So you killed them."

"I would have," Seruf laughed. "Sadly, they chose to flee. Except for Ellard, of course. Although he's little better than a human now."

"And I suppose you created me to ease your loneliness?"

Seruf's eyes widened, but her smile never faded. "My, my, you're more tempestuous than I thought."

I glared at her, my brain at war with itself. One part—the rational side—argued that I should choose my words more carefully. This was not a human crouched before me. Nor was it a hybrid. Seruf was a Celestial. Ageless and powerful.

The other part of me, the side that was battered, tired, and had grown a prickly defensive shell, told me to keep going. To see how she would react to my provocation. After all, what would she do in retaliation? Kill me? I no longer feared death.

Turn me into a Wraith?

Considering how ~~callisly~~ callously I'd viewed the destruction of this town, the transformation would hardly be traumatic. It didn't seem I had much of a soul left.

"I'm not tempestuous," I said. "Only truthful."

"Oh yes?" Her eyebrows raised. "You are a child. What truths do you know?"

"You created me," I said. My mind rolled back, and back, and back, recalling everything that had happened since Mama died. "Perhaps you intended to keep me, but something went wrong." I remembered the day of my transformation and the second Celestial who took me away. "I was brought to Sakar, where you were barred from going. And, for more than a decade, you did not try to reach me."

"Perceptive!" she exclaimed. "A true marvel! Yes, child, I abandoned you here, didn't I? It was not intentional, I assure you. When Ch—well," an angry twinge crossed her face, but she quickly smoothed her expression. "My brother will be dealt with…in due time, of course. But I was led to believe you had perished."

"'Led to believe?'" I repeated. "But had no desire to confirm?"

Another ripple of annoyance briefly marred her face. "I did not believe I was being lied to. And you cannot fathom my relief upon hearing you were alive."

My skin suddenly seemed stretched too taut over my ~~skelton~~ skeleton. It was uncomfortable. As was the churning of unease in my stomach. "Why did you not create another hybrid to replace me?"

"Creating hybrids is no simple task, my child."

"Why? Does it deplete your powers when you give a human a piece of it?"

Seruf straightened, her wondrous wings ruffling as she stretched and began to walk, allowing my question to go unanswered.

"Your shoes are terribly impractical," I said. She did, indeed, have the most ridiculous pair of boots I'd ever seen. The tops were open, exposing her foot to the elements. And the heel was so elevated, it forced her to stand on the balls of her feet. It was a wonder she could walk.

"Perhaps for these rudimentary human streets." Seruf wrinkled her nose in disgust as she scraped the toe of her silly boot across a patch of dirt. "But in Norhall, where our roads are even and well-paved, these shoes serve me quite well. You will adore Norhall, child. It's modern. And clean." Her lip curled as she regarded the ruined town.

"I'm sure this town was clean as well. Before you destroyed it."

Seruf made a small *hmming* sound. "A *clean* town? Where humans sleep side-by-side with their livestock—"

"Animals are great company."

"Child," she knelt before me again.

I tensed when she twirled a lock of my hair. Not because I feared her attack. But because her touch, unwelcome as it was, made my skin prickle, a sensation that usually accompanied the emergence of my power.

My apprehension was rather silly, of course. She was the Firestarter. My fire would not harm her.

In all likelihood, she would harm me.

But she didn't seem inclined to do so, as she worked the knots and snarls out of my hair. "Poor thing," she murmured. "What is your name?"

"Lass," I answered.

"*Lass?*" Seruf scoffed. "Oh no, no. My dear, that is not a *name*. That won't do at all."

My skin itched again. I could still hear Terrick's voice as he rolled my name off his tongue. "I've no desire to be called anything else."

"Well," Seruf combed her fingers through a freshly untangled section of my hair, "may I make a suggestion? What do you think of the name 'Lasair?' Do you know what it means?" she asked when I started to protest.

"No," I said.

Seruf smiled. "'The Bringer of Light.' *Lasair.*"

I turned the word over in my head. *Lasair.* It was similar to what Terrick had affectionately called me but more sophisticated. A better fit for an adult, perhaps.

"It's not all that different from Lass, is it?" Seruf said, as though she'd heard my thoughts.

I didn't want to admit I rather liked it. So I stayed silent as she combed my hair.

And perhaps I was a fool. Perhaps I was simply starved for a touch of kindness, but I relaxed beneath her ministrations. My breathing steadied. My tense muscles loosened.

She drew back, cupping my chin in her palm. "Would you like to see Norhall, child?"

I swallowed. *No.* The only word out of my mouth should have been *no.*

But I said nothing.

Seruf continued. "You are my protégé and you would be given the finest accommodations, afforded every respect and comfort. We have soft clothing." She traced a hand over the cuts and hives on my bare shoulders. "And warm, scented baths you can indulge in whenever you wish. And the *food*… have you ever tasted chocolate? Sweets?"

At my blank look, she tapped her fingers against my chin. "You will sample them," she assured me. "As many as you'd like. What say you?"

Bile rose in my throat.

At the time, I didn't understand why. She had shown no abhorrence, no inclination toward violence. Only a friendly, soothing demeanor.

Yet her touch, her presence, and the sweet apple scent that wafted from her skin made my stomach roil in rebellion.

Despite her caring words and gestures, there was no warmth in Seruf's eyes.

Aside from the power we shared, Seruf had no bond with me. She did not care for my well-being. If she had, she would not have assumed me dead so easily. She would have continued searching for me until she saw my corpse with her own eyes.

It's what Terrick would've done. For all the mistakes he made, Terrick never gave up on me. He cared too much to let me go.

Seruf didn't care.

She only wanted the fire that flowed through my veins. The fire that had come from her own blood. She wanted the piece of herself that she'd given up returned.

I would find no love if I accepted her proposal.

But perhaps I could find peace.

Seruf, far more powerful than I, would certainly not fear me, or look at me in repulsion as the humans had done. Could I live freely beneath her tutelage? Could I, perhaps, learn to control the fire that had long terrorized me?

A fluttering sensation rose in my throat. A peaceful life. It was all I'd ever wanted.

But what would that peace cost me?

The rolling sound of hoofbeats drew me away from my ponderings.

No less than a dozen human soldiers rode into Vaporia. They drew their snorting, panting horses to a halt, and grimly surveyed the debris surrounding them.

Seruf turned, her wings spasming as a flicker of annoyance crossed her face. The soldiers, likely blinded by the billowing clouds of ash and smoke, did not immediately see her.

"We're too late!" a man said as he dismounted his horse.

"Search the buildings," a woman called. Her horse shied when a smoldering ~~skelton~~ skeleton of a home collapsed, sending embers into the sky. The woman snatched the animal's reins, steadying it. "Move quickly. And bring the wounded to Quinn."

*Quinn.*

In my chest, the heart I thought had turned to coal fluttered.

There he was. *Alive.* Dismounting from his horse, his face ashen. He laid a comforting hand on the red-headed woman beside him as she shifted rubble off the burnt remnants of a child.

Quinn's brilliant blue eyes surveyed the rest of the ruined town. They paused when he caught sight of me. Widened. Realization dawned on his face.

"Seruf!" he shouted. "She's still here!"

Immediately, the red-headed woman drew her bow and fired her first arrow. Her aim was true: the head of the arrow struck Seruf's right shoulder. The wound oozed a silvery light —the same substance Seruf had forced me to drink when I was a child.

Seruf did not flinch when she wrenched the arrow from her shoulder and tossed it aside. Her irritation boiled; I could almost feel its heat.

She would kill them.

And I felt no remorse for them. Except...

Quinn stood still, even as those around him drew their weapons. Even as the red-headed woman fired three more arrows. Seruf avoided two. The third pierced the side of her throat but, again, she did not flinch.

Quinn still did not move. He seemed rooted to the spot; his eyes affixed to my face. The hurt and confusion in his gaze made my insides burn with shame.

Quinn had been the only human, except Terrick, who had not believed me to be evil. He helped me when others would have harmed me. And now he saw me with Seruf and was likely regretting he'd ever spared me a moment of benevolence.

But his kindness, passion, and even his arrogance had been the few dim rays of light in the bleak well of despair my life had become since leaving Swindon. I'd not known Quinn long. I'd not known him well. But, for some inexplicable reason, I cared for him. And I couldn't bear to see him perish.

He had saved my life once.

Now I would save his.

"Yes!" I said, even as another arrow hurtled at Seruf. This one missed her but clipped my left ear. I relished the aching sting it left behind.

Seruf turned to me.

"You asked if I wished to see Norhall," I said. "My answer is yes."

With a gleeful chuckle, Seruf pressed a lingering kiss to my temple. "You'll adore Norhall, child. Now, allow me to extinguish these pests..."

"Must you?"

"They shot an arrow at me. And at you."

"You were left with barely a scratch." Her wound had

already healed. "Against your power, humans are little more than insects."

"You pity them?" Seruf raised an eyebrow.

"As anyone pities a trodden insect, yes. Humans are wretched creatures, but they know no other way of being, so the fault does not lie with them. And..."

Quinn drew his sword. Unlike the other soldiers, who handled their weapons with ease, Quinn fumbled, nearly dropping his blade.

"I've grown tired of trodding on insects." My lower lip quivered. "I ask that you spare them. If only to spare me the revulsion of seeing yet another trampled creature."

A long, ~~eggaerated~~ exaggerated breath escaped Seruf's lips. "Very well. For you, my darling, I would do anything." She combed my hair, her fingers lingering against my scalp.

I tried to ignore the sticky sensation that coiled in my gut when she touched me. Tried.

*"Lass!"*

Quinn's voice pierced my heart.

As Seruf wrapped her arms around me and spread her wings, I caught a final glimpse of him. He'd forsaken his sword and was sprinting toward Seruf, ignoring the shouts and commands from his fellow soldiers. "Lass! Don't!"

I closed my eyes when Seruf flapped her wings.

And, thus, my time living amongst the humans came to a close.

My time with the Celestials began.


TO BE CONTINUED....

# Acknowledgments

It's time to get sappy, y'all!

My adventure with Addie and the crew began when I was 18
—nearly 15 years ago! I'm not sure when I got so old, lol. And
the idea came from a mix of things:
A.) I've always loved epic fantasies but didn't always love
reading them because the writing tended to feel a bit dry for
my taste (looking at you, *Lord of the Rings).*
B.) I've always skewed toward campy/cheesy humor and
wished more fantasies utilized that (like *Xena: Warrior
Princess,* which is 100% as campy as it is epic).
C.) I was a Catholic school brat (from a surprisingly non-reli-
gious family…but that's a story for another time, lol) and
angel mythology fascinated me.

Long story short: I wanted a dark/epic fantasy with badass
angel lore and oodles of campy jokes. And that was…not
what I wrote when I was 18, LOL. The plot was a mess, the
characters were cardboard cutouts, and I hadn't found my
voice yet, so the writing had as much personality as a slug.
But I did the thing and wrote an entire long-winded book, so
kid me gets an A for Effort. And that dumpster fire of a book
was the very first step on the long-ass stairway that led to
Fires of the Forsaken. Because as awful as my original version
was, it lived rent-free in my head for *years.* Because I *knew* my
idea was solid. It just needed better execution.

Fast forward *many* years later, and this story was still bouncing around in my head. So I decided to dig in. I re-read my originals, tossed the garbage, kept what worked, took the time to build the world properly, and flesh out my characters (impatient 18-year-old me did *not* do this). And, *voila,* the kickass story known as Fires of the Forsaken was born.

But I couldn't have reached this point without help.

First and foremost, I have to thank my mom. She read (and loved) the original dumpster fire version of this story and she's been my cheerleader through every step of this rewrite.

I've also gotta give a huge shoutout to my beta readers: Hannah, Stephanie, and JoJo for taking a chance on this wild story and telling me when I was running the plot in confusing circles. (And to anyone who might've read the original version *way* back in the day…thank you. It's been a while, and my memory isn't great, so I'm sorry I can't give you a personal thanks. But I am deeply appreciative of the feedback I got in my teenage years. It helped me find my writing voice.).

I can't do an acknowledgment without casting the spotlight on all my fellow Never and Ever Publishing authors. Publishing is a hard industry that has more downs than ups, so having a support system is crucial. You need people you can vent to, bounce ideas off of, cry with, and who will celebrate your success with you. N&E has given me that group, and I'm super thankful for it.

My editor, Meg, is a flipping rockstar. I dumped this book and 20ish pages of notes on her on New Year's Eve. I was like an unhinged and over-caffeinated creative sliding into her

DMs in the middle of the night, lol. But she muddled through my ramblings and, as always, provided crucial feedback to whip this story into shape.

Lastly, I have to thank YOU, the reader, who picked up this book knowing it was going to be weird as hell. *Thank you,* a million times over, for taking a chance on me and this wild story. It wasn't exactly lighthearted fare, but I hope you enjoyed the journey. And I know I left all my characters hanging in some rough spots, but they'll be back. I promise.

Playlist

1.  I Dare You – Shinedown
2.  Mad World – Gary Jules, Michael Andrews
3.  Monster Made of Memories – Citizen Soldier
4.  I Won't Let Go – Rascal Flatts
5.  Zombie – The Cranberries
6.  Vienna – Billy Joel
7.  What I've Done – Linkin Park
8.  Boulevard of Broken Dreams – Green Day
9.  Shallow – Lady Gaga, Bradley Cooper
10. The Lonely – Christina Perri
11. Monster – Cassie Levy, Frozen: The Broadway Musical
12. My Immortal – Evanescence
13. The Sound of Silence – Disturbed
14. I Am – James Arthur
15. Wolf Within – Jonathan Young, Caleb Hyles
16. Renegade – Styx
17. I Will Not Bow – Breaking Benjamin
18. Unravel – Jonathan Young (cover)

# About the Author

As a child, Stephanie E. Donohue roamed Narnia with the Pevensie siblings and rode the Hogwarts Express with Harry and his friends. She never tired of discovering new and magical worlds through the pages of a book. And, when the yearning to explore still wasn't satiated, Stephanie turned to writing. With a pen and a few sheets of paper, she learned to craft new worlds, and vibrant characters to explore with.

That passion has never died. Stephanie still enjoys writing stories that take readers on exciting, and sometimes dangerous, adventures.

When she's not writing, Stephanie can usually be found cuddling with her two cats, obsessively re-watching The Office, or rocking out to a Pound Fitness class.

# Other Books by Stephanie E. Donohue

**Standalones**

Windsong (2022)

Bewitched by the Sea Monster (2025)

**Across Time Trilogy**

Fires of the Forsaken (2023)

Ashes of the Earth (2024)

Embers of the Damned (2026)

**Across Time Companion Trilogy**

Hunted by Fire (2024)

Betrayed by Ash (2025)

Cursed by Ember (2027)

# More Books You'll Love

If you enjoyed this book, please consider leaving a review.

Then check out more from Stephanie E. Donohue
sedcreations.com

*She just wanted a gosh-darn pizza. The apocalypse had other ideas.*

Addie did not have "getting plucked from the 21st century and thrown into the apocalypse" on her "things to do after work" checklist. Yet here she is, trapped in the hellscape known as Sakar–a world torn apart by a Celestial war. Now she's dodging soulless Wraiths, getting chased by venomous horses, and trying her darndest to avoid a meltdown.

Thankfully, Cheriour, the gruff and grumpy commander of the human army takes her under his wing. He's blunt, brutal, and socially awkward. *Totally* not Addie's type.

So why does she find him so infuriatingly attractive?

As Addie's connection with Cheriour grows so does the danger. Wraiths threaten to eliminate the last dregs of humanity and secrets about Addie's past are about to surface that might just make her the key to saving everything... or destroying it.

**Darkly thrilling and laced with biting humor,** *Fires of the Forsaken* **is perfect for fans of** *Game of Thrones, Deadpool* **and** *Supernatural.*

*Earth's last hope has anxiety, a lethal power, and absolutely no idea what she's doing.*

Addie is having a colossally bad year. She's stuck in a bullshit biblical war, her friends keep dying, and her newfound power might be slowly eating her alive.

At least she has Cheriour, the gruff, battle-scarred commander of the human army, who is secretly a teddy bear hiding beneath a grumpy face. But even their budding relationship is threatened as the war rages.

With Wraiths scavenging the ailing country of Sakar, and the Celestials tightening their grip, Addie must lead a desperate mission to save what's left of this world. But the deeper she dives into the secrets of Sakar—and the reason she was brought here—the more she realizes some truths should stay buried.

**Gritty, emotional, and packed with sharp humor, *Ashes of the Earth* is a thrilling grimdark romantasy perfect for fans of *Game of Thrones, Deadpool* and *Supernatural*.**

www.ingramcontent.com/pod-product-compliance
Lightning Source LLC
Chambersburg PA
CBHW070504200726

48293CB00007B/2379